PRAISE FOR
THE AOSAWA MURDERS

Most Notable Books of 2020   *New York Times*

Best Mystery Novels of 2020   *Guardian*

"Strange, engrossing, stubbornly non-linear…"

New York Times

"Tantalising as a scene glimpsed through a half-open door, this is an utterly immersive puzzler in which nothing is entirely cut and dried."

Guardian

"Ms. Onda's novel—part psychological thriller, part murder mystery—is audacious in conception and brilliant in execution."

Wall Street Journal

"Rich and strange, utterly absorbing. Onda makes you aware of another, different world below the surface of this one."

The Times

"One of the most praised novels of the year. Can this book open up the world of Japanese crime in the way that *The Girl With the Dragon Tattoo* opened up Scandi Noir? I hope so."

Globe and Mail

"This dark and dazzling novel defies easy categorization but consistently tantalizes and surprises."

Kirkus Reviews

"It won the Mystery Writers of Japan Award for Fiction and was hailed as a masterpiece. I agree."

Mystery Scene Magazine

"Intoxicating details and shiver-inducing propositions hold the full story at a careful distance; when the truth emerges, it's both partial and staggering."

ForeWord Reviews

"The genius of this novel is that it cultivates a nonstop air of menace. Practically every character comes off like a potential murderer."

NY Journal of Books

Riku Onda, born in 1964, has been writing fiction since 1991 and has published prolifically since. She has won the Yoshikawa Eiji Prize for New Writers, the Japan Booksellers' Award, the Yamamoto Shūgorō Prize and the Naoki Prize. Her work has been adapted for film and television.

Fish Swimming in Dappled Sunlight is her second novel to be published in English. The first was *The Aosawa Murders*, which won the prestigious Mystery Writers of Japan Award for Best Novel and was selected by *The New York Times* as a Notable Book for 2020.

FISH SWIMMING IN DAPPLED SUNLIGHT

Riku Onda

Translated from the Japanese
by Alison Watts

BITTER LEMON PRESS
LONDON

BITTER LEMON PRESS

First published in the United Kingdom in 2022 by
Bitter Lemon Press, 47 Wilmington Square, London WC1X 0ET

www.bitterlemonpress.com

KOMOREBI NI OYOGU SAKANA by ONDA Riku © 2007 ONDA Riku

All rights reserved.

Original Japanese edition published by CHUOKORON-SHINSHA, INC., Japan in 2007

Republished as a paperback edition by Bungeishunju Ltd. in 2010

English translation rights throughout the world reserved by Bitter Lemon
Press under the licence granted by ONDA Riku, Japan, arranged with
Bungeishunju Ltd. through Japan UNI Agency, Inc., Tokyo

English translation © Alison Watts 2022

Bitter Lemon Press gratefully acknowledges the financial assistance
of the Japan Foundation and of the Arts Council of England.

A CIP record for this book is available from the British Library

PB ISBN 978-1-913394-592
eB USC ISBN 978–1–913394–608
eB ROW ISBN 978-1-913394-615

Typeset by Tetragon, London
Printed and bound by CPI Group (UK) Ltd, Croydon CR0 4YY

1

This, I guess you could say, is the story of a photo. Sure, it's also the mystery surrounding the death of a certain man, and a mountain tale as well. Plus there's the relationship aspect: the break-up of a couple. But the photo is at the heart of it.

Speaking of photos, I had a weird experience the other day. I went into a bookstore to kill some time before a meeting, and my attention was instantly captured by the cover of a book on display. It was a famous photo. Three young men, formally dressed, walking along a hard dirt road through fields. All three looking back over their shoulders at the camera.

They stared at me with looks that were hard to define. I know they were looking at the photographer, but something about the angle of their heads as they turned to look behind them made me feel like I was the one they were observing.

That photo happens to be part of a collection, one man's project at the beginning of the twentieth century to record the lives of people from all walks of life. I got a bit of a thrill to think that long after those young farmers had left this earth, their gazes travelled across time to meet mine in the twenty-first century. The most unsettling thing about it though was the sense of déjà vu. I felt sure I'd seen those expressions before. That this wasn't the first time several people had turned to look at me in exactly that way. I was certain of it, and it disturbed me.

But now's not the time to think about that. Right now I need to concentrate on the task ahead, and on the conversation I'm about to have. Because, as I've said, this is also the story of a man and a woman breaking up. I say that with total certainty because I'm one of them, and the woman is here with me. Tonight is our last night together in this apartment before we go our separate ways.

I left the window open on purpose. It sounds strange, I know, but I get a kick out of leaving the window open at night for the outside air to connect with the inside. It feels less confined, I suppose. And I enjoy the occasional puff of early-summer breeze coming through.

The movers have already taken most of our stuff, and the apartment looks bare. We sit on the tatami mat floor, facing each other over that suitcase of hers, which we're using as a table. There aren't any floor cushions left, but sitting on the matting feels nice and cool.

Naturally we don't have bedding either, so tonight we'll have to make do. Tradesmen are coming first thing tomorrow to stop the gas, water and electricity. Then we return the keys to the real estate agent, step outside, and each go our own way. That's the plan, anyhow.

These last few days have been taken up with packing and shifting, so we haven't had time for a proper talk. You never think of everything that needs to be done when you move, not until the last possible minute. You also never know how much you own until you start packing, either. It's amazing how much we had crammed into a modest two-bedroom apartment like this. We've been so busy sorting our stuff the last week that we've hardly even seen each other. But all along I think we've both known we'll have to thrash things out at some point. If we don't, neither of us can get on with our lives.

A nice breeze blows through the screen door. Soft on the skin.

This apartment is an upstairs one, on the corner of a building sandwiched between a small river and a children's park. I really liked living at eye level with the park trees, though the scent of Osmanthus could get a bit much in autumn. Sometimes it was so overpowering we couldn't taste our food. My room overlooked the park, so I could always tell the time from its clock pole.

"It feels so empty, doesn't it," she says.

A room with nothing in it should feel empty, but this room isn't completely empty. There's one object in here we're both doing our best not to see, but it's unavoidable, like a speck in the eye.

You can see marks on the walls and tatami where furniture used to be. They look like ghostly shadows of our things, reminding us of their existence. The light fixtures have all been removed, so there's only a single naked bulb for illumination. But it serves the purpose.

So, let the last supper begin. She's bought food and I've bought drink. We went out shopping for supplies once the truck loaded with our belongings had disappeared around the corner, but somehow we ended up going off on our own instead of together. We know each other's tastes, though. I got a bottle of the full-bodied red wine

9

she likes, and she bought the vermicelli salad and other stuff I like from the supermarket.

My hunch is that this will be a long night, and I'm sure she thinks so too.

She sets out cheese and olives, in anticipation of a long haul, and I put down a bottle of strong shochu and one of mineral water. The room fills with the smell of food, drowning the scented night breeze coming through the window.

I'm ready for this. The cool, collected part of me is prepared for the night ahead. She senses it, I can tell, from the tension in the air as we get things ready. The false peace we've managed to maintain is beginning to crack.

But we keep up appearances as we open cans of beer for a toast. And the smiles we exchange are genuinely intimate, despite the tension behind them.

"What a beautiful night," she murmurs, looking out of the window. Or is she thinking about something beyond the window?

"Yeah. Best time of year, I guess. Not long now before the nights get really hot."

"Oh yes. Remember how awful it was last year."

We make trivial conversation, both waiting for the right moment to begin.

Knowing each other as well as we do, we can read each other's feelings. Once there'd been a honeymoon period in our relationship, but then we fell into a pattern of conducting regular and intense battles of wills. These have become more frequent lately, leaving us both fed up with the endless warring. Another good reason to leave this place.

She hands me disposable wooden chopsticks. I snap them apart and we begin amiably enough, snacking on the food spread out on the suitcase table.

"Are you going anywhere over the summer?" she asks, casually.

"No plans yet. I'm busy with conferences and so on. I don't even know if I can get time off for a summer break this year," I reply, equally casual. "Aren't you going to Vietnam the day after tomorrow? That'll use up all your summer leave."

"Not all of it. I'm thinking of taking my leave in parts and going somewhere in September too."

Tomorrow she's going to stay with a friend, and the day after that the two of them are going to Vietnam together. This suitcase we're using for a table is probably packed with everything she needs for her break. I can see her standing on the beach now, wearing a Vietnamese ao dai tunic, her face hidden in the shadow of a white wide-brimmed hat.

I serve myself a helping of noodle salad and take stock of the situation: it's like a game of musical chairs, and we're in the process of circling to see who gets to sit on the last remaining chair. In our case, though, winning that chair won't result in any prize. If anything, we both want to be the last one standing and are each trying to provoke the other into sitting down.

"Your hair's grown long," I say.

She looks at me in surprise, then smiles slightly. "Have you only just noticed?"

"Haven't seen you much recently. In my head it was still short."

"I suppose I haven't worn it down for a while. It gets in the way when it's an in-between length, so I tie it back all the time."

She downs the last of her beer, flicking her fine, brown-tinged hair in the process. Her hair's been short all the time I've known her, but now it's long enough to reach her shoulders. It really is lovely – I like how the feathery line across her forehead frames her pale, delicate face. It's a shock to see her this close up, and face-on. I haven't looked at her from this angle for ages.

"How's that friend of yours doing?" she says, looking me in the eye. "What's her name again?"

Uh-oh. That caught me off guard. "Uh, she's okay, I think."

"It's all right. You don't have to hide anything," she says with a blank expression. "Say hello from me."

We both open another beer. She doesn't want to discuss the topic any further. I get that. The girl I'm going to live with is not on our list of priorities for discussion tonight. We have something far more pressing to talk about, a matter concerning just the two of us.

Where should we begin? Where does this story start? I guess I'd have to say it begins with that photo.

"I saw a movie the other day," she says, beer in one hand, turning her eyes from the window back to me.

I know she's avoiding eye contact. She only looks at me now and then, when she pretends she's suddenly remembered something. But I don't stop looking at her. Looking at her not looking at me.

"At the cinema?" I ask.

She shakes her head. "No, on television. It was one

of those late-night movies, an old black-and-white one. There were these university students sitting around in an apartment like this, not doing anything much and getting bored. Then one of them turns on the gas and challenges the others to see who can stay in the room the longest."

"That's suicidal. If they didn't kill themselves, they'd cause an explosion."

"They all seemed taken with the idea, and everybody went along with it. Whoever chickened out, lost. The winner was the last one left in the room. Those were the rules."

Quite the concept. "What happened in the end?"

"I forget," she answers simply.

"Was it a Japanese movie?"

"Yes. It was very short, less than eighty minutes, I suppose. Almost the whole movie was them in the same room, trying to withstand the gas."

"Humph." I stare at her, wondering. Did she grab a chair just now? Is this the beginning of the night? The thought sends a shiver down my spine. I sense a slight escalation in tension. To neutralize the feeling, I stand up in a rush.

"What's wrong?" she asks, looking at me.

"I forgot to buy cigarettes. I'll run out and get some."

She examines me briefly then turns her eyes away again. "Oh. Well, in that case, can you get me a bottle of iced green tea too?"

"Sure. Big or small?"

"Big is better. You'll probably drink some too."

"Sure thing."

I stuff my wallet into my jeans pocket and head outside, where a sudden urge to yell at the top of my voice comes over me, but I stifle it and take some deep breaths instead, sucking the humid summer air deep into my lungs.

The night folds gently around me. It feels good, almost sensual, and I hang around outside the apartment for a minute or two, enjoying it. Then I pull a squashed packet of cigarettes from my shirt pocket. The truth is I still have some left, but I needed to get out of there in a hurry – I had to escape her presence for a while. She picked up on that, of course. She knows I'm wavering and that the cigarettes are an excuse to get out and get myself together. I light one and walk off, dragging my feet. Calm down, I tell myself, this is your last chance. She probably did force you onto a seat just now. Let the evening begin.

She has to confess. I have to make her do that tonight.

The store lights come into view.

Can I do it? At some point during this night, will I be able to get her to say with her own lips that she killed that man?

2

At the sound of the door shutting behind him, I collapse to the floor. Not from tiredness; I simply can't bear this situation any more than he can. I'm suffocating, and I feel like screaming at the mere thought of the long night ahead.

Lying on the tatami at least feels good. Cool and pleasant. The room looks strange from this angle, empty of our belongings and with my own hair and arms part of the scene. Rooms usually look bigger once their furniture is removed, but not this apartment. It still feels awfully small. I don't know how the two of us managed to live here with all our possessions.

Goodness, that vermicelli salad smells. The whole apartment reeks of it. I don't know why store-bought food is always like this. It always looks so tempting on the shelf that I feel compelled to buy it, but when I bring it home I can never use it all. It's a good thing tomorrow is rubbish collection day. At least we can put it out in the morning when we leave.

If I turn my head, the suitcase that we are using as a table, with all its scratches and dents, enters my field of vision.

I'm not going to Vietnam. That's a lie, although it's true that Atsuko, my friend, is going the day after tomorrow.

I'm staying in her condominium apartment for a few days while she's away. She invited me several times to go with her, but I don't have the energy to be part of a group tour at this time. I've never liked group activities anyway. Even as a child I was always much happier left to my own devices. I knew the adults didn't approve of that, however, so I pretended otherwise. I think I managed to fool them. Having to spend time in the company of strangers has always been draining for me, and it would be too much of a strain to do that now, when I'm not exactly bursting with energy.

Atsuko's family is wealthy and she earns good money, so she can afford to live in a beautiful place. I look forward to being there on my own and doing whatever I feel like doing without having to talk to anybody. Once Atsuko leaves I'm going to simply lie around the whole time. I can't wait.

I picture myself there already, in the bright, cheerful condo with its white, gauzy curtains, lying stretched out on the wooden floor, exactly as I am now. It's strange to think that's where I'll be in less than twenty-four hours.

The curtains sway as something flickers and dances across them. They turn a soft, leafy green. I am in the forest, with bright rays of sunlight slanting through the treetops. One day this path too will crumble and vanish, a deep voice says.

With a jolt I open my eyes to find myself in the apartment on an early summer's night. Of course. The source of the glare is the naked light bulb dangling from the ceiling.

Cold sweat trickles down my back. Slowly, I raise myself up off the floor. That voice... it was *his*. I thought I'd forgotten it. But it seemed so clear it couldn't have simply been my imagination. For a moment I am frozen.

After-images linger vividly in my eyes. Green sun-stabbed shadows dance ominously in time with the beating of my heart.

I reach for my beer and gulp it down noisily, hoping that the crude sound will erase the flickering shadows from my mind. I take another mouthful, and another, until my stomach rebels and a burp erupts. The shadows vanish, but that's probably due more to an urge to urinate than anything else. Shall I give in to nature? I was planning to keep toilet breaks in reserve for when I need an excuse to pause the conversation. There will be times over the course of the long night to come when I need to step back and think.

The call of nature wins out and I stumble to the bathroom. There's an empty space where the washing machine used to be. In the mirror above the basin next to it I see the ghostlike face of a young woman and stare into her eyes. They remind me of the girl in the movie.

Why on earth did I bring up that movie? I can't even remember how it ends. It's just an old flick about a group of idiot students with too much time on their hands. I remember one scene where spit dribbles down the chin of a girl who looks strained and faint from the gas.

Maybe it's not so different from our situation, maybe that's why I thought of it; the two of us about to spend a night together cooped up in this apartment, tête-à-tête, risking our lives in an endurance match.

Back in the living room I sit down heavily on the floor, feeling like a puppet with my strings cut.

Endurance... This last year certainly has been an endurance test. That trip, and the death of that man, changed things forever for us. We were so close until that point, but those few days tore us apart. Ever since then, I feel like we've been walking on quicksand, sinking deeper and deeper with every step, not getting any closer to the place we want to be. I've been constantly on edge, my feet feel like lead, and I can't help always being suspicious, looking for evidence. Sometimes I catch myself sneaking glances at him, trying to read his eyes.

Leafy shadows flicker in a corner of my mind. Inside them, a figure walks uphill.

It's been like this since it happened: me suspecting him of having had a hand in that man's death. At first it was simply a vague unease, but over time my suspicions have grown, and now I'm close to being convinced. So much so that I can almost see the moment he killed him.

This scene has been occupying my mind a lot of late. I could be on my way to work, buying a bottle of cold tea from a vending machine, or doing the laundry, when it comes over me. The image is so graphic and clear that it always stops me in my tracks. Then I start going over things in my mind, all over again. But I have no intention of reporting him. The man is dead, and officially it was deemed an accidental death. My intention is not to rake up the past so it turns into a criminal case. All I want, all I desperately need to know, is *what* he was thinking.

Hello. I've heard a lot about you.

Another voice – *hers*. I see her petite face framed by a bob. She's a pretty young thing. Didn't he say she was also in the club at university, one of the junior members? A girl with dimples and no trace of make-up, a girl as wholesome as organic fruit. He's leaving here to go and live with her. She's already moved into their new place, apparently, and is waiting there for him now. When he told me that, I wished him happiness and asked why they weren't tying the knot. He thought about it for a few seconds before replying that they were planning to once things settle down. I've been wondering ever since what that means. What *things*? What must one do to *settle down* anyway?

Once things settle down…

Whenever I hear his voice in my head, I see his face with that tight-lipped, strained expression he often gets. He's like me – good at keeping emotions in check. I know, though, that the times he appears to be unreservedly considerate are actually when he is at his most agitated and trying to conceal something he absolutely should not say. I used to admire that talent; I identified with it and respected him greatly for it, but now his smile only fills me with terrible fear.

Ever since we decided to leave this apartment and lead separate lives, I've begun to feel afraid. I knew I couldn't live with him any more and was desperate to get out as soon as possible, but at the same time I dreaded that day arriving.

What would happen when it did?

I knew I wouldn't be able to leave without saying something. I can't leave if I'm still harbouring doubt.

Will he tell me the truth? And if he does, will he believe me when I say that I have no intention of reporting him? How will he process this in the cold dark recesses of his mind – the parts that I have no access to? From his point of view, he is embarking on a new life, and I am simply in the way. Therefore tonight is the perfect opportunity to make me disappear. I can imagine him saying it nonchalantly: Oh, I haven't seen her since we left the apartment.

The reason I keep talking about going to Vietnam, even though I'm not, is so that he will think twice about doing anything if he believes my friends will raise the alarm when I don't turn up to meet them. I want to live, even after we're apart. I want to see what life is like without him. And I can't stand the thought of him tying up loose ends by disposing of me and going off to start a new life with that girl.

I hear whispers in my head: *I'd sooner this night kill me. Let it put an end to my life.*

Mmm, it's so dark outside… the breeze on my face feels good, like an invitation from Death himself trying to tempt me.

That would be one way to end this.

Even as a child I was painfully aware of the impermanence of life. It was like an ache that I tried to ignore and distance myself from, as if it weren't part of me. Sometimes I want everything to disappear so I can erase my own existence. By dying, for example, or by saying goodbye. Those are possible endings I could choose. The world will go on regardless.

I crawl clumsily to the window and stare into the darkness through the wire screen. He sent that man to his death, and tonight he will kill me. When I'm dead and buried and my bones are turning to dust, he will still be living with that girl and the world will go on.

If my death turns out to be an outcome of this night, many small traces of it – the food we ate, and the conversation we had – will vanish like bubbles of foam. I feel an acute sense of transience, and recognize this mood that comes over me sometimes, suffocating me with its weight.

I inhale the cool air flowing through the window.

The small children's playground outside seems miles away right now. We used to treat it like a garden, an extension of our home.

We're alike, the two of us. So much alike, he once said. I remember how he crowed over that.

On nights when it was too hot for sleeping, he and I would go to the playground. We'd sit on the swings in the dark and drink beer. It felt so intimate. We said things there that we could never have spoken of inside. When we first started living together in this apartment we often spent hours and hours at a time, talking outside. I see his hair under the street light, the drink can in his hand dripping beads of moisture, and hear the faint squeak of the swing. Now would be a good time to sit there and talk about the events of a year ago, but the two of us will never sit on those swings side by side again.

When I was a child, I always used to wait for my turn on the swing. Now, however, it looks to me as if it is waiting, patiently, for somebody to come and use it. Maybe that's what growing up means – never having to wait your turn for the swing.

We've come a long way. How much further will we go tonight?

I hear footsteps and sit up straight. He's back, I can tell. I always know when he arrives home because my body reacts instinctively to the sound of his feet stamping up the stairs.

The doorknob turns and the door opens with a click.

"You're back."

I arrange my face into a smile, ready to greet the man who may be planning to kill me.

3

The bag of drinks is heavy. My hand has gone numb where the handles are wrapped around my fingers. Food and drink weigh a lot more than you think.

I learned that for myself when I moved out of home after high school and began living on my own. Being a poor student, I used to cook to save money. I never had a taste for fast food like most of my generation.

Potatoes, onions, cabbages, apples, salad dressing, canned tuna. This kind of food has weight, like a living thing. Shopping at the local supermarket taught me that, as I gradually got used to getting meals for myself. Luckily I didn't dislike cooking, and I bought in bulk when possible, so I could experiment with all kinds of dishes.

Once, when I was at a friend's place, I was surprised to learn that practically all he ever ate was instant ramen and prepared food out of a packet. He got a supply of these by playing pachinko, which he was addicted to, and took away his winnings in the form of instant foods. If he ever went shopping, he always came back with a bag full of cup ramen and potato chips. Things that have no weight, despite their bulk.

That's not proper food, you can't live on that, I

remember thinking once while listening to my friend rave on about a new kind of cup ramen.

"Hello there."

All the time I was standing in the dark lost in thought, she was observing me. A living woman.

I look down at my feet to avoid her eyes as I remove my shoes before entering the room. Compared to the sense of lightness and freedom outside, the atmosphere in here is deathly quiet and suffocating.

"Did you find cigarettes?"

"Yeah." I tap my breast pocket and nod. Then I pull the bottles of iced green tea and water from the plastic bag and place them in front of her. The bag is damp with beads of moisture.

"Oh, you bought mineral water as well? It must have been heavy."

"Yeah, I almost broke my arm." I unclench my stiff hand. Red marks line the palm.

"The walls aren't stained much, are they?" she says, leaning back on her hands as she holds her head high to look up at the ceiling.

The stains she's referring to are cigarette smoke. It's true: you can hardly see them even with the furniture gone. I guess they blend in with the wooden ceiling.

"I was careful. Most of the time I went outside to smoke, or over to the playground."

She doesn't smoke. Women don't like tobacco stinking up their hair and clothes. I used only to smoke when I had a drink, or to relax after work, and almost never inside the apartment, but this last year my habit's grown to the point where now I smoke more than a pack a day.

Ever since the trip. Smoking became my excuse to get out of the apartment after that. The amount of time I was spending in the playground rocketed, along with my cigarette consumption. It was to get away from her – I see that now.

She reaches for the plastic bag, folds it into a ribbon and knots it in the middle, like she always does. It's her habit to tidy away plastic shopping bags immediately after use, as they pile up so fast. The sight of her fingers moving automatically triggers a memory of somewhere else.

A woman in a blue checked shirt, doubled over in the long grass.

Her. She is alone, crouching in silence as her fingers move busily. She seems to be tying something – making some kind of trap, perhaps? That doesn't require any special tools. Just a simple construction on the ground to trip the feet will do it. Remove all traces of the trap afterwards and it looks like accidental death. Easy. I remember an incident that was in the news, about a group of students from a school nature camp. Somebody got up to mischief knotting pieces of grass together, which another student got their feet caught in while running around. There's always one joker who'll pull stupid tricks like that.

"Actually, I lost one of my earrings," she announces.

"An earring?"

"Yes. I think I dropped it while I was packing." She doesn't sound terribly upset.

"If it was a pearl earring, it'd be like that Yuming song."

"It's nothing that valuable. More like zirconia." She lifts her hair to show me her left ear. A tiny hole is visible where there's usually an earring. For some reason, the sight of that hole makes me uncomfortable. Its rawness reeks of intimate cruelty.

"Not the one you always wear?"

"Yes."

"When did you notice?"

"This morning."

She always wears a pair of inconspicuous earrings with clear stones. That's what she's lost. I search the floor around me.

"It's probably still in here somewhere. Something that tiny could easily fall through the gaps between the mats and you'd never notice."

"Or it might have fallen into one of the cardboard boxes." From the tone of her voice, it sounds like she's resigned to not finding it. "Now that you mention Yuming and 'Pearl Earring'…" she says, as if she's suddenly remembered. She shoots me a look.

I regret bringing up Yuming. Our situation is exactly like the one described in her song.

"I was arguing about the lyrics with a friend recently. You know them, don't you?"

"Yep."

In high school, I used to go out with a girl who was a huge fan of Yumi Matsutoya and had all her albums. I didn't think her voice was so great and couldn't understand her popularity, and then I listened to her first album, *Pearl Earring*. The lyrics, melodies and Yuming's style blew me away. She has this way of vocalizing that makes it sound like she's emitting ultrasonic waves. At first, I only listened to please the girl I liked, but I ended up borrowing all the other albums from her. So the answer is yes, of course I know the song 'Pearl Earring'. I remember it well.

"There's one line that goes: '*I threw one earring under his bed / Ah, pearl earring,*'" she sings.

Her voice isn't powerful but she can hold a tune, and I have to say that the song describes our current situation perfectly. There's another line that goes: "*You'll probably realize after you move in with that pretty girl…*"

"When the woman in the song is in the guy's bedroom for the last time, she throws a pearl earring under his bed," she continues calmly. "That's how it goes, doesn't it?"

"What about it?" I reply coolly, not wanting her to get an edge.

"The point is, whether the girl still has the other earring or not. That's where my friend and I disagree."

"In other words?" I still didn't understand her point.

She opens another beer and takes a sip. Apparently she isn't ready for wine yet.

"My interpretation is this. I think he bought the pearl earrings for her when everything was wonderful between them, and now that it's not, the sight of the earring only makes her think about what's coming. She knows that they will part, and that there is no hope of patching things up. His mind is already on life with another woman, so she thinks, I'll never wear these earrings again. I mean, even men wouldn't wear something a former girlfriend had given them, no matter how expensive, or how much it suited them." She looks me directly in the eye.

I force a wry smile and nod.

She flashes a brief smile in return and continues. "That's why she decides to dispose of the earrings. I expect she chose a place with special memories to do it – somewhere by the sea perhaps, or maybe the spot where he gave them to her – and she throws one away there. Then she goes to see him at his place for the last time, and leaves the other one under his bed. So now she doesn't have either earring any more. That's my take on it."

"Okay, I get it." Her argument is convincing. "She threw the remaining earring under his bed."

"Yes." She nods, pleased that I understand. "But my friend insisted that it's more usual to interpret the words literally – as in, I threw away only *one* earring."

"So she still has one earring in her possession. Hmm. She does have a point."

I have complicated feelings about this discussion. I'm amused and impressed by their analysis, but it scares me how much emotion those girls invest in discussing Yuming's lyrics. I remember when her "best of" double album was released. I was on the bullet train on a business trip and saw a number of women, older than me, listening to that album, all completely lost in their own world, which freaked me out.

"But there's another line that comes afterwards," she says sulkily. She doesn't like that I sided with her friend. "'*Some things are no use if the other half is lost,*'" she sings. "That means that there's no point in keeping one earring when the other is lost, doesn't it?"

I'm sceptical. "That could be interpreted another way – I'm not myself now because I left half my heart with him. I think that'd be the straight interpretation."

"Hmm. You're surprisingly romantic." She stares at me, looking genuinely surprised. "You can live with someone for years and still not know things about them," she mutters, as if talking to herself.

You can't know everything about a person. If anything, it's easier to count the things you do know. I mean, you can't even know everything about yourself. I can't say I know anything about her. I used to think I did, but now I don't feel confident any more.

There was a time we used to feel like we were the other's half. And I really think we were for a time.

She stares out of the window and I stare at her left side in profile like it's a mysterious object. That tiny hole in her left ear makes me wonder about the right. If one earring of the pair she always wears is lost, what will she do with the other?

"Hey, what happened to the right earring?" I ask. "Did you get rid of it?"

She laughs, then gently covers her right ear and slowly turns to look at me. "What do you think?"

I'm being tested. What she actually wants to know is what am I thinking. I hear the man's voice whisper in my head: *Some things are no use if the other half is lost.*

4

I know I am right about 'Pearl Earring'. Women are able to put the past behind them and get on with life, while men have to use strategies like turning to historical novels. Men look back at the past and count women as conquests, while women are concerned only with looking at the present and future.

Some women do drag their pasts around, and I don't deny that I have that tendency too. But I usually keep that part of me closeted away in a separate room: the guest room, so to speak, where the guest can feel sorry for herself at leisure. Only occasionally do I invite her into the living room and allow her to wallow in self-pity to her heart's content. Self-pity is merely entertainment for women.

In any case, I wouldn't keep the remaining earring – except in a situation like this.

It's only half true that I lost one of my favourite earrings. The other is in the leather sling bag that he keeps for casual use. He has it with him now. I stare at the worn, amber-coloured bag at his side. It reminds me of a small animal at rest. That's where my earring is, deep in the corner of the outside pocket.

We both like bags. Why else would we purchase new ones every season? We were suckers for the latest bag with a nifty pocket or functional compartment. But during everyday use, all those supposedly useful pockets turn into black holes that swallow things up. That quickly becomes clear when one loses something and searches through the pockets to find it. Movie ticket stubs, taxi receipts, cardigan buttons, precious addresses scribbled on scraps of paper: all these things that once seemed so important, which we turn the place upside down searching for, surface like faded, scuffed flotsam cast up by waves on the beach. Once recovered, the items no longer seem useful or essential, and end up stuffed away somewhere, never to be seen again.

Last night, I deliberately placed one of my favourite earrings deep in the pocket of his bag.

My heart is thumping. Maybe this is what it feels like to set a landmine or a trap. The pocket of the bag looks almost glowing to me.

I wonder when he will notice. Maybe tomorrow. Maybe in a few months' time. Or maybe he never will, and the earring will be disposed of along with the bag. I can see that happening. The aged, blackened leather bag, pocked with holes where it's worn away, perched on top of a pile of waste put out for collection.

Why did I do such a thing? Was it out of sentiment, or for insurance? I don't understand it myself, and I stare at him thoughtfully.

He looks preoccupied, because he's wondering if I still have an earring in my right ear. I love that earnest expression of his, the one that comes over him when he is thinking deeply about something. It's tinged by shadows. As if glimpses of a melancholy that is ordinarily well controlled slip through the defences around his heart.

He once said, while watching me carefully ponder something, that he could hear the sea. At the time, my only thought was that it was a poetic thing to say, but thinking back on it now, I feel as if he might have been pointing out an inner turbulence in me.

Which makes his deep consideration now like a beam of light. A single beam shining deep into quiet darkness. Casting light on nobody.

"You're wearing it," he says, pronouncing the words decisively.

I smile, then remove my hand covering the earring in my right ear. The hard stone has left an imprint on my fingertip. "Bingo."

Seeing the zirconia in my ear silences him for a second, then his face relaxes into an expression of relief. "I'm glad." He reaches for the bottle of wine.

I look around for the plastic cups and opener. "Drat, we don't have a corkscrew." Too late; I remember packing it.

"It's okay," he replies, pulling his bag close.

I draw a sharp breath. He opens it casually and scrabbles through the contents, then fishes out a folding army knife. The knife, which he always carries, is equipped with tools such as a can opener and scissors. Being Swiss, it also has a corkscrew.

He didn't even touch the pocket containing my earring.

Watching him deftly open the wine, I feel the tiniest bit hurt. The disappointment of a woman when a man fails to notice her new hairstyle. This is one possible scenario I had not thought of.

As he pours me some wine, another interpretation of 'Pearl Earring' occurs to me: the possibility that despite the woman successfully casting the pearl earring under the man's bed, he is not perceptive enough to notice it among all the bustle and confusion of moving, because the bed has not been shifted in years and beneath it the floor is cloaked with layers of dust. At least, my own grain-sized zirconia earring would not be noticed. All this thinking is making me dizzy.

"What are you smiling at?"

"Oh, nothing." Suppressing my smile, I hand him a cup and pour some wine into it. "Why did you think I'd still be wearing it? Despite me having just said I thought the woman in the song threw away the other earring."

It is his turn to smile. "You may be twice as cool as most people, Aki, but you're also twice as sentimental."

I grimace wryly. There was a time I would have been overjoyed to hear these words, but why is it a stab to the heart to hear him say it now?

He immediately notices my reaction and allows me a glimpse of faint regret.

"Don't spin me that line – the same goes for you." I give him a bright look, daggers in my eyes, and gently wipe the mouth of the wine bottle. "We're alike, you and I," I add. There's a bitter taste in my mouth all of a sudden. Hastily I take a sip of wine. He does the same. A gentle breeze slinks through the window as if to try and appease us both.

Feeling suddenly weary, I sip my wine in silence. He drinks his, and toys with the tip of the corkscrew on the dark-red knife. If only we could wind this up quickly and get things over and done with, I think. His long white fingers continue to stroke the corkscrew.

A sense of déjà vu comes over me. This scene is familiar. Where have I seen it before?

"Want some cheese?" he says. He looks over at the supermarket bag, as if he's just remembered it.

Does he really have no idea what he is doing with that corkscrew? His constant stroking of its sharp, pointed tip gives me the creeps.

"Yes. What about you, Hiro?"

"I'll have some salami."

At last he stops playing with the corkscrew and takes the stick of salami from the bag. His favourite, the one with hot black pepper. My sense of déjà vu grows stronger as I watch him deftly slice it.

I have seen something like this before. Rays of filtered sunlight shoot through my mind. Green flickering shadows.

"That time..." The words slip out without thinking. "Why didn't you use the knife then?"

"Huh?" He looks at me with a hard expression.

Sweat was pouring down the both of us as we trudged up a steep incline. Though it was still early summer, the weather in the S— Mountains was unexpectedly fine and clear, and all indications were that the day might turn out to be the first hot day. We weren't walking in direct sunlight as the trail wound through thick ancient forest, but this trek was no walk in the park, and we were panting. I was perspiring so much I wondered how on earth a body could contain such volumes of liquid. My eyes stung from the salt and my shirt was encrusted with it.

Not surprisingly, our expert guide and leader was not at all out of breath; in fact, he'd hardly broken a sweat. He may have been a mountain guide while we were office workers who spent our days indoors in air-conditioned environments, but it was embarrassing to think that he was in his mid-fifties while we were only in our twenties. Nevertheless, we managed to ascend a hundred metres in one spurt and came to a level section of the trail. Noticing our breathless state, the guide suggested taking a break.

We nodded, unable even to speak, then lowered our backpacks to the ground and wiped our faces with the towels wound around our necks. My body burned fiercely, although the sweat had a cooling effect. I gulped down water but could not quench my thirst, and my body cried out for something else to satisfy it.

"How about an orange?" Hiro said, reaching for his pack. He must have been thinking the same.

"Sounds good."

One of my colleagues who was a keen trekker had told me, "Oranges are best on the trail. They take away the thirst but don't fill you up so much with water that you need to take a piss straight away." That's why I had brought some, although I had completely forgotten giving them to Hiro to carry. He extracted one from his pack and fiddled about with it.

"What are you doing?"

"I'm trying to divide it up, but it's not working out."

"Shall I peel it?"

"It's hard to peel because of the soft pith." He tried digging his nails in for a while, but he didn't seem to make much progress.

"Here, use this." The guide, who had been standing surveying the area, pulled out a well-worn knife and handed it to Hiro.

"Thanks." Hiro opened the knife with a practised motion and cut the orange into four quarters, then handed the guide and me a quarter each.

The orange was warm, but its citrusy scent eased the fatigue and the juice damped down my thirst. "This tastes amazing," I marvelled.

Hiro made sounds of agreement as he sucked on his piece of orange, then he sprinkled some water from the drink bottle over the knife to wash off the juice before wiping it clean with a towel.

"Thank you very much," he said, returning the knife to the guide.

"Didn't you have your knife with you that time? I saw you use it later on. When we got back to the lodge and you cut up the salami."

My eyes travel to his hands. We had eaten this same salami then, too. He stares at me with a strange expression, still gripping the knife and salami.

"You've got a good memory to recall something like that."

"I just remembered." I notice that my voice is hoarse.

Was that a note of emotion I detected as he spoke? I consider the possibility. Could it be anger perhaps, or venom, or agitation? Did I imagine it?

He stares at the knife like he's never seen it before. "That's right. You're right," he mutters, as if to himself. "I remember that too. I was trying to divide up the orange by hand because I didn't have my knife then."

"But —"

"That day," he says, interrupting me, "the knife wasn't where I usually keep it. Somebody must have taken it from my backpack before we left, then returned it to the same place later. I swear to it."

I don't believe a word of it.

5

I stare at the folding knife in my hands. Her face can only be described as pale.

The knife. I'd completely forgotten it.

She's right about it disappearing from my backpack that day. At the time I didn't think much of it. I assumed I hadn't looked carefully, but thinking about it now, I can only conclude that it was removed from my backpack for a period during the day.

But it's strange. By evening the same day it was back again. And the man fell to his death, so it wasn't like the knife had been taken to stab him. So why did someone remove it? I don't understand. And why did she bring up the topic anyway?

I begin to slice the salami in silence. She is still pale-faced, staring at my hands.

"You took it, didn't you, Aki."

"Me?" She sounds wronged, and her face looks angry.

"Well, who else could it be?" She's the only one who knows I always carry a knife.

"Why would I take your knife?"

"I don't know. Maybe you wanted to use it for something, and borrowed it from my pack then forgot to return it. Isn't that what happened?"

The blade is sharp beneath my fingers, gouging into the salami. It feels good. A pungent black-pepper smell shoots up my nose.

She shakes her head emphatically. "It wasn't me."

"Think about it – who else could it be besides you? We hardly saw anybody."

"Uh-huh."

She can't disagree with my logic and is stuck for words.

We planned out a leisurely schedule for that trip together. First we took a train to A— prefecture and spent the night at a well-known hot spring resort where the water bubbles up in the sea. Then next day we met our guide, an expert on the World Heritage Site S— mountain range. Our first day with him we did some light trekking, then next day he took us on a trail through an area dotted with lakes. Apart from the guide, we didn't say anything to anybody that you would call a conversation. And we only spoke very briefly with the manager at the lodge. If my knife was valuable, I might understand. I can't see anybody risking discovery to steal it.

She is deep in thought, with her fist against her nose. "It doesn't make sense," she says eventually, "but it wasn't me."

"It's weird."

She looks at me sharply. "If you didn't use it, then only one other person could have taken the knife. On our second day of trekking."

I have the same thought. "Him? It couldn't be. Why would he take my knife?"

Our guide was sturdy and looked much younger than his age. It was only natural he was in better physical shape

39

than us, because of his job and living out in nature. But he also had a kind of urbane air about him. He was good at putting people at ease and made a favourable impression on me.

"We look forward to the next two days," I said to him.

"Thank you for coming. I hope you'll enjoy the tour," he answered in a precise, polite tone. "Let's get you used to it gradually."

That wasn't our first encounter. We'd met the previous day at our hotel to discuss plans; however, he gave off a different impression outside in the mountains. Maybe it was his relaxed manner in comparison to our nervousness. In any case, city slickers like us stood out there, while someone like him who worked in that environment blended in.

It was still early, but there wasn't a cloud in the sky and the air had already dried out. You could tell it would be stifling hot in a few hours' time. This was before the climbing and holiday season, and on a weekday in early summer the area was quiet. There was hardly a sign of human presence, and the densely forested mountains were intimidating. You got the feeling of a raw ancient power that could wreak terrible revenge if offended.

The forest began to stir, and we held our breath as we entered the trees. The first place our guide led us to was a strange, beautiful lake.

"Divine," Aki murmured.

The deep blue lake looked extremely cold. Its blueness came from minerals in the surrounding earth, cobalt I guess.

"It reminds me of night," she said.

The guide looked pleased. "It does. There's always a starry night sky in there."

Although it was beautiful, that lake made me feel afraid. Like I might see something I shouldn't if I looked into its depths.

"We had a beer together that first night, didn't we?" she points out in an even voice. "He would have had access to your pack then. We were both tired, and while we were off making phone calls and buying beer, our luggage was unattended."

Rays of light from the setting sun shone through the large window in the lodge, where we sat at the end of our first day, going over it and discussing plans for the next. We shared a general sense of relief as we said cheers over a glass of beer.

"I was worried at first, but you turned out to be a couple of good walkers. If you haven't got it, you haven't got it – even if you're young. A lot of young people these days have weak ankles." Our guide didn't drop his formal tone with us even after spending the whole day together. I guess that was his style.

"But we won't feel the stiffness until the day after tomorrow," Aki said with a laugh.

"Do you play any sport?" the man asked.

I nodded. "I played tennis all through high school."

"We met through the tennis club at university."

"You two seem to get on well. It's not often I see young couples trekking together in the mountains."

"Is that so?"

We exchanged glances and then invited him to our room for a drink, since the discussion looked like it might continue for a while. He refused firmly at first, but accepted reluctantly when we insisted that we needed to go over the route for the next day.

In the room we discussed our plans, but also mentioned more personal things. Though he spoke little, the guide began to make a few personal comments too.

I cut up salami and cheese with the knife and offered them to him. He took some and said thanks. I asked if he had been born in the area. He shook his head and replied, "Tokyo."

He told us that he'd been a keen trekker in his youth and regularly visited these mountains. When his company mentioned transferring him overseas, he decided to quit and move here instead. He'd been single since divorcing when he was young, but had married a much younger, local woman after moving here and had recently had a baby.

"Oh, congratulations," said Aki with a big smile.

The guide blushed. "I never expected to be a father at my age. I'll have to keep working hard for a while."

It occurred to me how tough that would be. By the time his child came of age the man would be in his seventies.

"If it's your first child, I'm sure you can't help thinking it's the cutest thing in the world."

"I have to admit, he is cute. More than I ever could have imagined." The guide was beaming with joy.

"Do you have a photo?" I asked. Doting fathers usually carry a photo of their progeny.

He looked shy but couldn't hide his delight as he pulled a photo from his top pocket.

"How old is he?"

"Nearly two."

The photo showed a cute baby boy in the arms of a chubby, healthy-looking woman.

"What's his name?"

"Shinichiro, written with the character for forest."

"That's a fitting name for the son of a mountain guide."

"He's so sweet," Aki said.

I was acutely aware how self-conscious the guide seemed to be as the pair of us gazed intently at the photo.

"He could have taken the knife then, you know. But why would he have done? He had his own knife with him."

"We're discussing opportunity," she replies curtly. "You didn't use your knife any more that first evening, did you? If it was taken then, you wouldn't have noticed it missing until the next time you went to use it."

"True."

We'd had all kinds of things spread out on the table in our room: guidebooks, maps and various other bits and pieces. I'd intended to put the knife away, but if somebody had slipped it into their bag or pocket at the time, I probably wouldn't have noticed.

"But why would he do that? Maybe he took it by accident."

"Could anyone with such a well-used knife as his mistake it for a newer one like yours?" She glances at the knife in my hand.

She's right, there isn't much opportunity to use a knife in daily life. I find its multifunctional design attractive, but truth be told, I do kind of carry it around as an accessory.

"Why take somebody else's knife?" she asks herself. "For what purpose?"

This is starting to make me feel weird. Why is she so fixated on my knife? Is she trying to deflect my attention, perhaps? Is it a ruse to dodge my attempt at getting her to confess? But she appears to be deadly serious, and genuinely puzzled by the mystery of the knife. Or does she have some other purpose in mind?

She lifts her head and looks at me. "He might have noticed."

I react with a start. "Noticed what?"

"About us."

I see a sober glint in her eyes that chills me. They remind me of that lake. A lake like night, with stars always floating in it. A lake you shouldn't look too deeply at.

"No way. He couldn't. Did you pick up on anything?"

"No, nothing," she admits readily enough.

That's a relief. "Exactly. It's impossible."

But she still swivels her head from side to side. "Something just occurred to me. A reason why that man might have stolen your knife."

"What?"

She thrusts her hand out at me without a word.

"What?"

"Show me the knife, please."

I fold up the blades and hand it over. Gingerly she opens the scissors, corkscrew, can opener and blades, one by one, then stares at it. She must see something there, because her expression gradually hardens.

"Just as I thought."

"What is?" I quickly ask. I don't know why, but my heart is pounding.

"That he had his suspicions about us," she answers, bleakly. "I don't know what triggered it. Maybe because we were so keen to see the photo of his baby. But he was suspicious. That's why he stole your knife… it has to be. He must have noticed something when you were using it. When do you steal somebody else's possessions? When you want to know more about that person, that's when."

She gently pushes the knife back to me, with the tools still opened out. I stare at it – at the writing on the blade.

"The guide must have noticed your name engraved on it. And he stole it so he could confirm something."

I see my name on the blade, engraved in fancy letters, like the epitaph on a gravestone: CHIHIRO T.

6

In the empty room I look down bitterly at his knife, glinting ominously beneath the glare of the naked light bulb. It calls out to me, exhorting me to touch it. His name, engraved on that mesmerizing blade, is like a scratch that cannot be removed.

I see light. Not sunlight through trees. But a dull light, reflected off the knife. And a vivid image of that man drawing out the blade and looking at the name. It is dark and his face is hidden in shadow. Only the knife in his hand stands out clearly. He slowly traces over the letters with his finger. Finally he sighs and gently folds up the blade.

"I wonder when he noticed." The hoarse voice, I realize, is my own.

"There's no proof. No proof it was him. No proof the knife was taken at all." Despite this protestation his pale face betrays him.

For one thing, he himself has just said that the knife was missing at the time. Maybe he's noticed the contradiction, as now he is staring vacantly at a spot on the tatami.

I cannot erase this image from my mind, of the man holding the knife. His back is broad and solid. The solidity of it adamantly rejects my question. Neither his facial expression nor his emotional state is being conveyed to me.

I break out in a cold sweat. How can I be finding out now, on our last night together?

I gulp the remainder of the wine in my cup. Keep cool. Stay calm. Think it through, one more time.

Doing my best to be calm, I say, "If it was taken from your backpack, it would have to have been on the first night, wouldn't it?"

"Or the morning of the second day."

We stare into each other's eyes, seeking an answer there.

A warm breeze blows through the open window.

This is a different kind of silence than previously. Something is starting to shift between us. If that man had known the truth about us, then it casts a completely different light on the events of a year ago.

Tonight was supposed to have been for us, but now it is as if there were an intruder, creeping up on us stealthily from the past.

"I wonder what first raised his suspicions? Do you think he suspected from the start?"

"That's impossible." He lifts his head to look at me angrily.

"It was a coincidence. We didn't know when we made the reservation that he would be assigned as our guide."

Hiro had booked our trek through the Guides Association, a local government-affiliated body.

"You reserved by telephone, didn't you?" I ask.

He nods. "I made all the arrangements over the phone."

"Did you give out any personal information?"

I am starting to sound like a prosecutor. Hiro looks annoyed.

"I didn't say much. Only that we were both office workers and not in top physical condition, so we didn't want to do anything too difficult. I also mentioned that I'd wanted to see the area for a long time and was really looking forward to it. All harmless stuff. You heard me speak."

"What about your name?"

"We did that together, remember?" He cannot hide his irritation. "We paid cash for everything. We didn't rent a car, or use a credit card. I wouldn't have cared if we'd used completely false names, but Takahashi is common enough, so I reserved as Hiroshi Takahashi – only changing my given name. Less chance of slipping up that way. Plus I made all the arrangements from home, on the landline, so they couldn't have seen my real name. Unless someone deliberately set out to check it, which would be another story. It wouldn't take much to find out, if they wanted to. But we were just tourists. Why would anyone go to the trouble of checking up on a pair of trekkers coming by train for an inexpensive tour? That's what we both decided, right?"

Of course I remember. It was supposed to be a bit of fun, a diversion.

The S— range in Tohoku is home to the largest primeval beech forest in the country. These mountains in north Japan had long held special significance for us. *Someday we'll go there*. We hadn't actually said the words, but we had both thought it.

We often used to go away together, just the two of us. It was a way of making up for the blanks in our past. Wherever we went we had a good time and enjoyed each other's company. It was refreshing.

We didn't have much money and we both liked walking, so often we simply wandered through strange towns, deep in discussion of all manner of topics. I have a collection of pictures in my mind, like stills from a movie, of our time spent in this fashion.

A tiny quiet village in a mountain valley. He is leaning against the balustrade of a stone bridge over a fast-flowing mountain stream and reminiscing about his childhood. Dusk comes early in the mountains, but we are so absorbed in conversation we don't notice it growing dark, and we then hurry to find somewhere to stay. Stumbling through the dark along unfamiliar roads, we ring the doorbell of a house to ask the way.

Or the two of us, wearing rain capes, walk along a path through wide fields still bare after the last harvest. On this windless day the warm rain hardly bothers us. If anything, we are revived by the gentle mist-like moisture and feel reinvigorated as we deeply breathe in the signs of spring rising from the ground. It feels as if we could walk forever.

Yet another time we are on a country road rushing to find shelter from a sudden evening shower. We come across a bus shelter, a tiny hut, where we take cover, and we stand in silence with towels over our heads, staring at drops of rain dripping from the eaves.

These moments seem so distant, perhaps because we were happy then. They weren't so long ago, but we will never see those sepia-coloured landscapes again.

He was always browsing through guidebooks on the S— mountains. I knew about it, of course, but I never attempted to look at them with him. Instead, I used to flick through them on the quiet, when I was alone. We avoided speaking openly about our mutual interest in those mountains and our yearning to see them.

The subject came up one evening at the end of summer, in the clear balmy dusk while we were leisurely having a beer and discussing where to go next. Naturally we were aware of what was in each other's mind. The ancient beech forest soared in our imaginations like a far-off goal. And yet neither of us could bring ourselves to mention it.

We both knew that it would be our end point. For a long time we'd known that day would come, but we'd had no idea in what form it would arrive.

Then came a portent. I still remember it clearly. It was winter. One night at the beginning of winter. He had a new scarf. A tasteful light-grey scarf that suited him very nicely.

"Oh, what a lovely colour, where did you buy it?" I asked, casually reaching out to touch it. It was like soft spun sugar, shot through with shiny threads.

"Er, I got it the other day," he answered, flicking it out of my reach. My hand hung in mid-air with nothing to grasp on to. I felt forlorn and empty, as if a window were being closed on me.

In that instant I knew for certain. Somebody had stolen his heart. A somebody who had given him this scarf. Clearly, he also thought a great deal of her. Which was why he had not wanted to let me touch it. I wonder if he saw then what I felt.

In any case, from that day on we began to draw apart, little by little, which he must have been aware of.

Then came the next change in the seasons. It was a drowsy, almost unsettlingly bright evening as spring approached. We were drinking beer, and finally the mountains came up as our next destination. And so it happened that last summer we went there.

I'm not sure where the idea came from to change our given names on the reservations. There were a number of guides, and the chances were low that we would be assigned that man. We set out on the trip wondering which straw we had drawn.

Looking back, we were so innocent then. Our minds were filled with bittersweet, childish fancies, like a pair of small children cooking up mischief. It was supposed to be private entertainment for us, to enjoy the intimacy of giggling over it together.

If we were lucky, he would be our designated guide. Coincidences do happen.

But although the thought was there, I don't think either of us expected it.

"That's right. I gave my name as Akiko Takahashi – we were Hiroshi Takahashi and Akiko Takahashi."

We usually call each other Hiro and Aki. So although the names we gave were false, they weren't so far removed from our real names as to make it difficult to use them with ease. Even if he did happen to be our guide, we didn't want him to be aware of our true identities. That was something we had talked about beforehand. To anyone meeting us for the first time, we looked like any ordinary couple.

This trip was supposed to be for the sake of personal memories, nothing more. We never even entertained the thought of him becoming part of our lives.

Of course, the S— mountains were significant to us in the first place because he was there. I'm not certain now where we heard it from or who told us; it seems as if we'd always known he was a guide there. But that fact wasn't of particular importance. We hadn't ever met him. He wasn't part of our lives, and if he hadn't existed at all it wouldn't have made any difference to us.

However, we did occasionally enjoy raising the subject of him. It gave us something to feel special about and share, our own modest drama featuring us as characters.

It would be a lie to say that we didn't hope for some kind of drama when we decided to go on a trip there. But it was the sense of drama that we were looking for, or the possibility of it anyway, not a drama itself. We know that now.

Yet that was what awaited us. We became characters in a drama that we were supposed to watch only from the sidelines. One that threw us into confusion, and which definitively tore us apart.

"If you knew – if we'd known…" I hear myself say hoarsely once again. I sound like a ham actor, tired of being a character in this drama yet with no choice but to keep on performing until the final scene. "Who on earth killed him – or, I should say, why did he die?"

He looks at me with a fleeting expression of fright, before calmly asking, "But didn't you do it, Aki?"

I look him in the eye.

There is a charged silence.

Who drove that man to his death? A man we met for the first time on that trip. Our father.

7

Chihiro Takahashi and Chiaki Fujimoto. These are our names. Takahashi is our mother's maiden name. We were raised together until the age of three. Then Chiaki's surname changed when she went to another family.

Mum never said much about it. She came from a poor background and suffered from health problems after we were born, though, so apparently she had no choice but to give up Aki.

People are different when it comes to their stockpile of memories. I have a friend who claims he has a perfect continuous recall of his life since the age of two, which is kind of hard to believe. Another insists he remembers almost nothing about primary school, which is also hard to believe.

I consider myself fairly average. I have little recall of kindergarten or before that, and my memories don't start to connect until primary school.

To be honest, it hardly seems real that I once had a sister. Though when I think about it, I do have a feeling there was another kid in the house when I was little, but I grew up as an only child, and by the time I had any real awareness of the world, I'd come to believe it must have been one of the kids from the neighbourhood.

Chiaki was the same. She'd also believed she was an only child.

What I do remember about Chiaki is her shoes squeaking when she walked. She didn't seem convinced when I told her, though.

"I did? I don't remember," she said.

"You know, those shoes babies wear that squeak when they walk, so the parents can keep track of where their kid is," I told her. "You were always on the go, running around all over the place, so I remember hearing that sound a lot. They were pink shoes, with thick soles."

Chiaki doesn't remember. But Mum did say she could never take her eyes off her because she was always running off and disappearing. She must've been the kind of kid whose attention was always captured by what she saw, who didn't notice the sound of her own shoes.

Chiaki, on the other hand, says I was a crybaby. When I object that I was no such thing, she just grins and says my face was always red, and whenever I didn't like something I'd throw myself on the floor in a tantrum. Every time she says it I get embarrassed and back off. It's like she's telling me I don't know myself very well.

Mum remarried before I started primary school. I adjusted to my new father easily enough. It didn't feel strange because I'd never known my birth father, not even from a photo. My stepfather became like a real father, and even after I found out we weren't connected by blood, to me he was still my only father. By complete coincidence his surname was also Takahashi. It's a common name.

Sometimes I wonder if my mother married him for that reason.

When I asked Chiaki about when she'd become aware of being adopted, she told me she'd always somehow known, ever since she was little. She had a vague sense that her family was different in some way. Which didn't mean she felt any the less wanted for it. As she grew up, her parents made sure to impress that on her with every milestone, so by the time she reached adolescence she was at peace with it.

I've met her parents. They're good, solid people, and welcoming to me. Chiaki tends to be introverted, but they understand her completely and accept her for who she is.

As to why my mother gave up one child for adoption, well, it seems that her feelings on the subject are complicated. She rarely mentions it, but did once let slip that she'd wanted to bring up both of us herself and shouldn't have given Chiaki away, no matter how tough things were. So it's clear to me that she always regretted it.

There was something else that always troubled her, which I didn't find out about until I was twenty. And that was that our father didn't know about our existence.

Mum doesn't like talking about the past, so it was a long time before I was able to grasp the whole story. In essence, when they separated he didn't know she was pregnant. Apparently he was a free-spirited sort of guy, who didn't like to be tied down. He'd married with the idea that it would settle him, but that didn't last long. He was a born wanderer, the kind of man who's always on the move, who can't even imagine staying in the same place for a month, so he was almost never at home.

This fits the image I have of my birth father: a travelling man, always alone, tramping along country roads, a backpack on his shoulders, drinking in the scenery.

Mum, for her part, can be downright stubborn and uncompromising. I guess she decided to separate because she couldn't stand the uncertainty, and once she'd decided to leave, she didn't even think of using her pregnancy to try and hold him down. She never told him about us and after the divorce was finalized, they never saw each other again.

Father had always been difficult to contact, even before the separation, and she never knew where he was, or how to reach him. She handed him the divorce papers when he came home to recover after an injury, but she didn't receive them back until six months after he left.

I was in university by the time I heard all this from Mum. And by then I had already met Chiaki.

"Me?" She gives a thin smile. There is an angry sadness in her eyes. "Are you saying I killed him? Is that what you think?"

It's clear she's experiencing some kind of emotion, but I can't identify it. We're always unconsciously trying to read each other's thoughts. Are we friends, comrades, family or sweethearts? We send out feelers into the other's head, probing and absorbing. And yet I don't know what I sense in her right now. Criticism? Hostility? Deep mistrust?

I have an image of her in my head that I cannot shake. She is crouching in grass, busily doing something with her hands. They move nimbly, tying blades of grass together.

"Am I wrong?" I reply frostily.

She smiles wryly. "I was convinced that you did it, Hiro."

This is a surprise. "Me? Why?"

She pauses. "Let me see," she says, and makes a show of thinking, then gives a slight smile. "Allow me to correct myself. To be accurate, what I thought – hoped for, in fact – was that you did it."

Despite myself, I laugh at the unexpectedness of this. Loud and relaxed. Now it's her turn to look puzzled.

"What's so funny?"

"I was just thinking: that's what this is all about."

"What what's all about?" she says, looking suspicious as she pours more wine into her cup.

"I was hoping the same."

I gulp down the rest of my wine. She immediately pours me another.

My head feels unusually clear, even though the alcohol is finally starting to affect me. That drunken sensation – of a thin membrane between me and my surroundings – is welcome tonight.

We've experienced our thought processes running along the same lines numerous times since we met. But I never thought that the similarity would run this deep, and that even in this situation we would think alike.

It's true I hoped she had done it.

The guide's death came like a thunderbolt from the blue. I couldn't have imagined anything like it happening, nor the unexpected rift it caused between us. It made our lives a mess.

I need a satisfactory explanation for his death. Something to allow me to file it away in my memory and be done with it.

That's how I arrived at this wonderful theory that she killed our father. That, to me, was the most plausible explanation.

"Why did you hope the same?" I half mutter.

"How can you ask that? Of course you know why," she swiftly responds with a glare.

I hold her gaze for a short time, then back off and look away.

"Of course you know why," she repeats.

It goes without saying that I know. I just don't want to put it into words. I say nothing and take another sip of wine. It won't be long before my lips turn dark. Why does the reflected sight of wine residue on lips always come as a shock, like discovering the aftermath of a crime?

I don't know.

I glance out of the window and see the trees swaying gently in the summer night. And the clock in the park that I must have seen hundreds, no, thousands of times before. Its hands are a painful reminder that the night is slipping away, minute by minute.

I don't know. Are we guilty? What is sin or crime anyway? I've never thought about it as much as I have the last few days and all of today.

"It might have been an accident." She sounds resigned. "A mountain guide slipping and falling to his death. That's all. Only this guide happened to be our father. Pure coincidence, along with the fact that we happened to be there.

Maybe we're simply trying to force an interpretation of murder onto something which isn't that."

I don't know.

I don't know what we've done.

I don't know if we're mistaken.

She pushes a strand of hair gently aside. "I thought you killed him, Hiro," she continues, "to give us something that would bind us together forever. Something we could never escape from." She looks me in the eye again. And once again I am the first to turn away.

"We're brother and sister, so we're already connected forever, aren't we?"

She laughs scornfully at my feigned innocence. "Oh yes. We're brother and sister, aren't we," she repeats, staring at a point on the wall. "Brother and sister for life."

A suffocating silence, thick with guilt, fills the air, smothering the icy suspicion that prevailed up till now.

I know this silence. It filled the chasm between us for hours on end during the most painful period of my life, ever. Up until now, that is.

She stands up slowly and heads for the bathroom.

I am staring at the clock in the park when I hear the door shut.

Bright, spring sunshine. Shiny, new green leaves.

From a long way off, she runs towards me.

She's right, I want something to tie her with. Something so powerful it can never be broken as long as we live.

A bitter taste rises in my mouth.

Whatever happens, there is no escape.

What is sin? Is it wrong to fall in love with somebody?

I slam my fist into that suitcase of hers. Paper plates loaded with snacks jump in the air.

I cannot lie to myself. Until we became aware of our kinship, we were in love.

8

In the dim light I scrub my hands vigorously under the running tap and peer at my reflection. My hands turn numb from the cold water as I continue to hold them there. How do I appear right now?

Is that really what my face looks like? Though I have seen it in this mirror a thousand times before, it does not feel as if it is mine. I reach out to touch it gently in the glass. It looks weary, the strain and fear starting to show. When we first moved here it had been so innocent and filled with hope.

What fools we were. We didn't see the trap we had set for ourselves – we hadn't seen it coming at all.

By the time we began living here we had already discovered our kinship and had convinced ourselves that we understood what that meant. He and I had both been raised as only children, so sharing this place was supposed to be a way for us to regain lost time with the sibling we had never known. Plus it was cheaper and more convenient to share with somebody in Tokyo, where the cost of living is so high. And it's much better from a safety perspective, too. At least that's what we told ourselves, and that was how we were able to convince our respective parents.

Mine were against it at first but came round in the end. They gave up when I informed them that I was an adult and could do as I pleased. Thinking back, though, I suspect they did not give the real reason for their opposition, and for the faint uneasiness in their eyes.

People often talk about a quirk of fate. For us, however, it was nothing to laugh about. It was a seemingly impossible coincidence that we should both have gone to the same university and joined the same club. But that's what happened, and the fact that it did gave us a sense of having been marked by fate.

Naturally we were non-identical twins, since we were male and female, but despite not being genetically identical, our characters and dispositions were very similar. So too were our academic results, hobbies and subjects in high school, and we were probably drawn to the same university because people with similar traits tend to do similar things.

When we joined the tennis club, each of us noticed the other immediately. The only way I can put it is that I had a feeling about him. He says it was the same for him. We're alike even in that.

Our tennis group was more a social than competitive sports club, but we did play seriously nonetheless, and practice sessions were rigorous. We had both played tennis in high school, and when we were paired with each other for doubles at the spring training camp, we were able to intuit each other's movements so easily you would never have known that it was the first time we had played together, much to everybody's amazement, including our own.

That's where we made the mistake of thinking that maybe this was love.

He made the first move.

The club was a big one, and large boisterous drinking parties were the main form of social interaction. But we began seeing each other in private after the first summer.

I rarely ever saw him on campus, as we were in different academic departments. One fresh, green summer's day, however, I bumped into him completely by chance. He stood out clearly among the crowd of students on the move, and I can still vividly recall seeing his mouth open in surprise when he spotted me.

That bright summer day of leafy-green light and unclouded sky is sealed in my mind forever. A day like that doesn't come twice. Without a doubt it was the springtime of my life.

The fact that we were both single was the deciding factor, I expect. He asked me out for coffee, I accepted, and we went to a quiet coffee shop a short distance from campus.

I had butterflies in my stomach as I sat looking at him across the table. I liked his intellectual appearance, his air of composure, and marvelled at the sense of intimacy between us. No doubt he felt the same.

I think we were both searching for the reason this feeling existed as we made trivial conversation about club gossip and our studies. Naturally we spoke of our upbringing, where we'd grown up and gone to school, and talked about high school tennis, but it was as if we were being careful to limit the topics of discussion, as if we knew that we shouldn't dig any deeper. We both had an intuition of something between us, that we were tied to each other somehow.

If that was the beginning of love, we thought it couldn't be helped. We were very young.

I wipe my hands on the towel and take a few deep breaths to steady myself, then I return to the living room.

He is still sitting there drinking wine with sullen, set eyes. I find it difficult to believe that this is the same man I saw that bright summer's day. It seems strange that there is an unbroken stretch of time connecting that moment to this. We certainly have travelled far.

"It must have been an accident," I say, sitting down on the tatami. "It's a good thing it wasn't treated as murder."

"Say he did know about us – when did he find out?" he says, speaking as if to himself as he stares at a point on the tatami, not looking at me. "I know Mum never told him."

I reach for the green tea, open the bottle and pour some into my cup. "That's the question, isn't it? He told us that he'd had his first child late in life. It didn't sound like he knew about any children with his first wife."

"Well, even if he did know, it's not something you'd talk about with clients you'd just met."

"But something must have given it away. Something which provoked him into taking your knife and wanting to know your real name. Perhaps he *did* know there were children. He might have heard it on the grapevine. But even if he had, why would he think to connect that with us?"

He looks deep in thought. "Because we asked him to our room – it has to be. We could've been too obvious about our interest in him. It wouldn't surprise me if he thought there was something going on."

"He would know from seeing your knife, at least, that you weren't using your real name. And from that he might have concluded that you were only hiding your real name because you were his own child."

Hiro leans over to grab his bag, and drags it towards him. I remember with a start the earring in its pocket. But as I expected he pulls out his Filofax without noticing the earring, and extracts a photograph from inside it.

"Ah," I exclaim. "You carry that around?"

"Yeah. I dunno why, but I can't throw it away."

He lights a cigarette and stares at the photograph. It's one I have seen many times. I have a copy too. It shows three people walking through the forest: me, him and that man.

"First and last shot of a father with his kids," he murmurs.

"It certainly is," I agree.

Three smiling faces turned to the camera. The smiles of a team of fellow travellers, temporarily together in place and time. The passer-by who took this photograph for us would never have guessed we were parent and children, because we were all putting on a performance.

It had been the off season and there were few people about, but on day three we saw several other tourists along the trail, I suppose because it was an easy route through forest, with lake views, and was generally fairly flat. We were stopped by a family who had asked us to take their photograph for them, and in return they took this one of us.

The three of us had been bluffing. Despite us being a family of father and two children, the photograph makes us out to be a young couple from the city with their local guide.

"You don't think it was suicide, do you?" Hiro asks. He sounds uneasy.

"What?" The idea shocks me. "Why would he commit suicide? He'd just had a baby. Didn't he say he'd have to work hard from now on?"

He shakes his head feebly. "You tell me. It's just a feeling. Maybe he hated himself for telling his other children – us – about it or something. Because he'd always denied our existence, so to speak."

"That wouldn't have been like him. I don't think he was the type to regret things."

"But sometimes people get overwhelmed by fits of despair and self-hatred."

"Do you, Hiro?" It sounded like that's what he was saying.

He looks startled by my question. "Don't you, Aki?"

It is my turn to be surprised at the bleakness in his eyes. Is it my imagination, or was there a faint note of anger in his voice?

Not to be outdone, I deliberately force a bleak expression into my own eyes. For a brief moment I can feel the darkness in both our eyes drawing us together.

"I do," I hear myself say.

Aha, that's one way, I think. Privately, I am shocked by the thought that this too is an option; we can both die here, tonight, if we choose. Our deaths would be because everything has become too much, because we have allowed the wretchedness in each other to trigger profound despair. It's become a thing for complete strangers to commit suicide together. Nobody would blame us if we did something like that. Who would find us? The person from the gas company? The real estate agent coming to pick up the key? I picture the scene. Bright morning, sunshine streaming through the window. The two of us lying toppled over each other next to the suitcase. That person, whoever they are, running from the room in panic.

What would people say? Nobody would know the depth of our hopelessness, though my parents might understand. Perhaps the hint of worry I saw in their eyes when we moved in together was an indication that they had already got wind of the trap we were falling into, and the misery that awaited me. That's right, my parents are capable of that. Maybe their instincts told them that their daughter could die of despair over a love that could never be consummated.

"Do you remember that time?" Hiro asks, reaching for the green tea. Perhaps he needs a break from alcohol. He fills his cup and gulps it down thirstily.

My thoughts have wandered off again without my noticing. "What time? When?" My brain isn't functioning properly.

"I'm talking about the time he fell."

This blindsides me, and I almost click my tongue in irritation. I hadn't expected him to raise that topic. The moment I learned that our father had fallen off a cliff, on a bright early-summer afternoon, has completely disappeared from my memory. I have tried hard to banish that scene.

Nevertheless, part of me always knew that I would have to recall it sometime. Not to mention that I always knew there would be no escaping it tonight.

"Not that well," I slowly reply.

"We were having a rest at the time, and all three of us were in different places. Which meant it was a while before we realized there'd been an accident."

So that's why. That's why I suspected him of the crime. He probably has the same suspicions about me, because at the time of the accident neither of us was in the other's line of sight.

He raises his head to look me in the eye and asks, "Come to think of it, didn't he say something about phones just before we took that break?"

"Phones?"

"Yeah. What was it... ringtones or something like that? I know – songs used for ringtones, that's what he said."

9

Piecing together fragments of memory is not easy work.

We've reached a point where all the memories I have of being with her lie smashed to bits. Painful even to recall, let alone attempt the extremely difficult task of connecting them with that trip. But that's what we need to do.

We haven't ever talked about what happened that day, which ended in a man's shocking, unforeseen death. Neither of us wants to rehash it. So going over things now won't be pleasant.

Sometimes it happens, though: something can trigger a memory and bring back the past in vivid detail. Since our earlier conversation about the knife, I've been feeling like the dam holding back my memories is starting to crumble. When I saw the photo, the events of that day came rushing back.

The weather was fine and summery. It felt good to be trekking through the soft green light of the forest along mostly even terrain. There was a bit of uphill walking involved, but nothing like the hard slog of the day before. The two of us were feeling good, wrapped in the kind of satisfied silence we always fall into when we're walking in a beautiful place. With every rise and fall of the ground we came to a different view, and the trail was easy walking, with twists and turns that took us past colonies of ferns and rare flowers. There was never a dull moment. It was like forest therapy, and we were drunk on the effects. We were like kids, gazing in wonder at the amazing forest and nodding enthusiastically at our guide's explanations. The trees concealed small ponds and lakes that appeared out of the forest like jewels, one by one, as if by magic. They were hypnotizing.

In the middle of all that, what was I thinking about as I followed behind the guide and Aki, staring at the speckled green shadow patterns on their backs? Well, I was thinking about Misako. Or, to be accurate, thoughts of her floated into my brain while I was thinking about Chiaki and me.

Misako Kawamura had also been in the tennis club and was two years below us. By our third year Chiaki had all but stopped going to club events, and she didn't know Misako.

Misako was a completely different type. In a nutshell, I'd say that where Chiaki is intellectual and sophisticated, Misako is straightforward and natural. I was intrigued by this unpretentious girl. But one of my mates had a big crush on her, and he used to drag me along with them to coffee shops and bars.

Although Misako was good at tennis, she didn't seem like the type for the tennis club. She was out of place in the fast, hard-drinking crowd, something she herself seemed aware of. Originally she'd joined the more academic archaeology club in the literature department, and ended up going back to that. So she was really only in the tennis club for a year, and her relationship with my friend didn't last long. I remember him complaining when she dropped him.

I'd almost forgotten she existed when I bumped into her again, completely by chance, the year before that trip to the mountains. I was in a large bookstore near Tokyo station, where I'd gone to look for reference materials on my way back from visiting a client. I've always liked bookstores anyway, and enjoy browsing the shelves of genres I'd normally never look at. Sometimes I buy a book on the spur of the moment, especially if it stands out visually, like a photo collection.

Misako was standing in front of a shelf in the store. I didn't notice her at first, but I immediately remembered her when she called me by name. She still had the same intriguing air about her. Now she had a good position as a senior researcher in the Ministry of Education, Culture, Sports, Science and Technology.

I had a bit of time before my next appointment, one thing led to another, and we ended up having coffee. Misako also seemed like she wanted to talk.

The conversation flowed easily and was surprisingly interesting. Talking face to face with her over a table was not like the days when she used to sit diagonally opposite, next to my friend. It was a novel, refreshing encounter that made me see a different charm in her. Misako apparently felt the same. It's a cliché, I know, but we both felt something click. I was aware, deep down, that I was searching for the opportunity to get away from Chiaki, and wanted this coincidence – Misako's reappearance in my life – to be that chance.

Inevitably, Aki and I had got ourselves trapped in a situation we couldn't get out of. The fact we'd pursued it ourselves didn't make it any less painful.

It wasn't like that at first. In the beginning we could say honestly to anyone and everyone that we were attempting to reclaim the family time we'd been denied. We had the right to live together as brother and sister and talk with each other about anything and everything. We might have even overdone it a bit with the drama of our story.

Gradually, though, things began to go awry. This weird kind of tension developed between us. Neither of us really understood why. Had we simply become used to each other? Were we getting tired of each other? I think both of us were secretly puzzled, and though we tried hard to erase the tension, it never completely went away.

Meanwhile, the days dragged on uneasily. We didn't speak about the situation. For one thing, we couldn't find the right words. It wasn't like any kind of problem we'd had before.

Then came that night.

It was a Friday, and raining hard. Midnight came and went, with no sign of the rain stopping.

Chiaki had gone out with her colleagues and was late home. Although normally she can hold her drink well, that night she sounded drunk when she came stumbling in through the door. I was working in my room and heard her come in, but then she immediately went quiet. I thought it strange that I hadn't heard her go into her room, and since I'd decided to go to bed myself anyway, I went out and headed for the bathroom.

She was sitting in the kitchen, with her coat still on and slumped face down on the table, motionless. I stood rooted to the spot. The sight of her felt ominous.

"Aki? What's up?"

She twitched slightly at the sound of my voice. "… I drank too much," she mumbled.

I was relieved to hear it. "Do you feel sick? Want some water?"

"Please," she said listlessly.

I went into the kitchen and took a bottle of mineral water from the fridge, poured a glass and turned around to look at her.

She was staring at a point on the table, her eyes open wide. The expression on her face gave me a jolt. She wasn't drunk. If anything, she was more in control than normal, but was obviously affected by something. I saw her eyes were red and realized she had been crying.

"What's wrong? Did something happen?" I placed the glass on the table and sat down opposite her. She looked pale.

Slowly she swivelled her head from side to side. "It's nothing."

"But you're crying."

Only when I pointed it out did she seem to notice her own tears. Though she hurriedly wiped her eyes and rubbed her face, her eyes stayed fixed on the table.

"Bad news?"

When I peered into her face she opened her eyes even wider and then shook her head emphatically. I didn't take that at face value, of course. I'd never seen her so upset before.

"We promised we could talk about anything, didn't we?" I said, encouraging her. That's what we'd decided when we started living together.

"I can't say," she said weakly.

"But you made a promise," I said, pressing her. I had to know what was upsetting her – I couldn't stop.

Even then she wouldn't budge. It was also the first time she'd ever refused to look me in the eye.

I started to feel uneasy. I waited. I needed her to answer, no matter what.

At last she gave in. "Yuji proposed to me," she muttered.

I was not expecting that. It was like a punch in the face.

I was taken aback not so much by the fact of the proposal, but by the terrible shock hearing about it had given me.

"And?" I asked. My voice was hoarse. I was confused and unable to figure out why I was so upset. Desperately I tried to control my agitation.

Yuji Takashiro had been in the year above us at uni and in the tennis club too. Aki had been seeing him for nearly two years. He was a good, solid guy, the ideal marriage partner, and I'd noticed that he seemed to love Aki deeply.

She shook her head.

"You said no?"

"I haven't answered," she replied sombrely.

This was some relief.

"To tell the truth, Yuji has been badgering me all along," she continued, keeping her eyes downcast.

"Asking you to marry?"

"No, telling me to move out."

"Of here?"

"He says that I shouldn't live with you. It's always annoyed him."

"Why?" My uneasiness grew. A feeling of dread crept up my spine.

"He said," she continued bleakly in a subdued, trembling voice, "that to look at us, nobody would ever think we were brother and sister, that it looks more like I'm shacked up with a boyfriend than a brother. He said that he can't stand me living with you."

I was stunned. A current of fear ran through me. For one thing, it was a shock to hear that Takashiro, who knew us, saw us this way, but the worst thing was realizing he'd hit the nail on the head.

I sat there lost for words, until eventually she raised her head and looked me in the eye. A chill swept through me. She'd never looked at me this way before. She radiated a dark sensuous aura. Her face was crumpled in anguish, and tears glistened in her eyes.

I broke out in goosebumps. In that moment I experienced an unnameable fear. I was forced to recognize that it contained not only horror, but also a peculiar thrill. In that moment I was also triumphant.

"I can't go with Yuji," she whispered tearfully.

She looked sublimely beautiful beneath the kitchen light. More beautiful than I'd ever seen her before.

"Hiro, you're the…" she began, then flung herself down on the table and started sobbing, her whole body shaking.

I was rooted to my seat, still speechless. What an idiot I'd been. The truth came crashing down on me at last. Takashiro had read the situation correctly. What Aki and

I had was not familial love. I might have wanted to believe that, but the truth was, we were in the grip of romantic love. And now that she was looking at me with those eyes, I realized that I, too, was looking at her as a man.

From then on, our life gradually became a living hell.

10

Whenever his eyes go distant like that I see sunlight flickering through trees. Fragments of the stifled emotion and desire that we do not put into words flit across them, like shadows woven through the wavering light.

Deep below the dappled sunlight, fish twist and turn at the bottom of a dark-blue pool. Occasionally they rise to the surface with a flick of fins, but it is impossible to see them clearly or count them.

I know he is remembering that night. The one that destroyed and set us definitively on the course that has brought us to this point.

It was a rainy Friday night. Wet and windy, cold and unpleasant. Inside my shoes my stockings were wet and chafing, and my hair was a complete mess. I was in an ill humour as I walked through the streets at night with the collar of my coat turned up, but my mood was not solely due to the weather.

I had been to a work dinner with my colleagues and had left after two hours to meet Yuji at a bar. He was already drunk when I arrived. When I saw his broad back from behind, I could tell he was irritated and in low spirits.

I hesitated for a second. I didn't know why, but I had the urge to turn on my heel and go home. Before I could do anything, though, he looked around and saw me, so I gave a small smile and sat down next to him.

He, too, was smiling, albeit uneasily.

Nervously, I ordered a gimlet.

I'd never spoken of this to Chihiro, but he had become a serious bone of contention between Yuji and myself. I originally met Yuji through Chihiro, who knew him from the tennis club, where Yuji was the senior and treated Chihiro like a younger brother. When I met Yuji I felt an attraction, and we started dating.

But Yuji's knowing Chihiro gradually came to be a millstone. He persisted in wanting to hear about my life with Chihiro. Although I never brought it up myself and tried to convey in a roundabout way that I didn't want to talk about it, he wouldn't stop. If I did tell him anything, he was always moody afterwards.

I knew that he was jealous of Chihiro but didn't take it too seriously. I remember in high school how I myself had been jealous of the younger sister of a boy I liked. I envied her being in the same house as him, speaking with him every day, and breathing the same air.

Yuji's jealousy was of a different order, though, and it was a small thing that brought me face to face with this fact.

One weekend we went out for dinner in Ginza and were on our way to a bar afterwards. We passed a small backstreet store specializing in imported foods, which was still open despite the late hour. By chance I saw in the store window some crackers that Chihiro liked, and they were reduced in price. The savoury crackers, flavoured with pepper and chilli powder, were a favourite of Chihiro's and he often ate them with a drink. But he had complained that the importer had changed, and the crackers had disappeared from the shelves of the local store.

When I saw them I said to Yuji, "Wait a minute," and went into the store to buy a box of the biscuits.

"What did you get?" he asked when I came out.

Without thinking I replied, "These are Chihiro's favourite."

I can never forget the look on Yuji's face. His gaze sliced through me like a knife. His expression was like a ball of fire, shot through with jealousy and hatred. I could not move.

I don't think it lasted too long. Once he registered my fright, his face immediately relaxed. Yet the moment I was pinned by his glare felt interminably long. I knew he was angry with me.

We continued walking, and I broke out in a cold sweat. I felt guilty and fraught, and hung my head. Like a woman caught in the act of being unfaithful. That's what Yuji's eyes had been saying.

"I'm sorry," Yuji mumbled in a tight voice, not looking at me. "I know it shouldn't bother me, but I can't stand it. You living with another man."

His voice was low. I could still see the fury in his profile.

"It's not like that," I protested. "We're brother and sister."

"No, you're not," he snapped. He turned towards me. Our eyes met directly, and I flinched. This time, Yuji did not attempt to shrug off his expression. Though his eyes had regained their usual composure, I glimpsed an iciness in them that wasn't usually there. "No, you're not," he repeated, slowly shaking his head. "The only ones who believe that, or, I should say, try to convince themselves of that, are the pair of you."

"You must be joking." I tried to laugh, though I couldn't pull it off. Yuji's assertion had shocked me deeply, but in my innermost heart I wondered if perhaps he might not be right.

We didn't discuss it any further. The atmosphere between us at the bar was now strained, and after a drink or two we left.

After that, the subject of Chihiro did not come up again, but our not talking about him – or rather, not being able to talk about him – made his presence grow even larger.

I grew afraid of Yuji.

By conventional standards he is the ideal partner, I suppose. He has the kind of looks and personality that gain him wide acknowledgement as a worthy and fine young man. In addition to his intelligence and geniality, he is understanding, a skilled conversationalist, and has strong leadership qualities. He exudes a good upbringing. He's the kind of young man liked by his elders, and he works for a top-ranking company where he is expected to rise into the ranks of management. Other women were always envious of me when I said I was going out with him. Yet little by little I came to find all that worthiness and perfection quite frightening.

His lack of flaws, and always being so even-handed and *right*, made me feel small and petty in comparison. Whenever I heard anyone praise him, I felt a pang of some strange, warped emotion that I could not put into words.

He only ever brought up his suspicions about Chihiro the one time, and afterwards I never saw it in his eyes again. Maybe he was putting on a show, but I do think he trusted me.

Over time, however, those clear, bright eyes pained me. If he had continued to air his doubts about me, I might still have thought to try and escape. If he had shown any jealousy at all, it might have been a reason to leave. But Yuji did nothing of the sort. Instead, he chose to show he trusted me, and continued to be the perfect partner.

Apparently he was telling other people indirectly that he intended me to be his partner in life. It was disconcerting to be congratulated by people I'd never even met before, teased by my university friends and envied by other women.

Looking back now, I can see his method of fencing me in. As long as I maintained that my relations with Chihiro were merely that of brother and sister, he would continue to prove that he was the perfect partner for me, and I would have no excuse to break with him.

I was cornered.

The situation began to cast a shadow over my relations with Chihiro. I could see that he sensed I was on edge, and I soon became aware of tension between us.

For a long time he seemed to be wondering what was happening, but he never said anything. If he had asked me I wouldn't have been able to answer, and I had no intention of trying to either. I suppose he was also assuming that I wouldn't give him any explanation.

But every time I noticed him looking askance at me or saw worry in his eyes, my heart ached. At the same time, I was annoyed with him for not divining my situation despite his keen intuition, and felt disappointed.

Ever since Yuji's outburst in Ginza, I had found it hard to behave normally with Chihiro. My own awkwardness exasperated me, but I couldn't help it. Every contact with Chihiro set off Yuji's voice in my mind, saying, *No, you're not.*

On weekends, when Chihiro and I watched television and drank beer in the evenings, laughing and talking nonsense, I could hear Yuji in my head saying: *The only ones who believe that, or, I should say, try to convince themselves of that, are the pair of you.*

Sometimes it sounded so clear and loud that I gasped.

"What's up?" Chihiro would look at me and ask.

"Oh nothing," I'd reply and smile wryly, feeling the blood drain from my face. How many times had that happened?

No, you're not.

The words tormented me.

At night when we said goodnight before retiring to our rooms, or in the mornings when we left the apartment together for the station, looked over at each other from opposite platforms and lifted a hand in farewell, Yuji's words came back relentlessly.

At first I desperately denied the possibility, then after a while I became tired of denying it and tentatively began to consider it.

Did I really love Chihiro as a brother?

I was in no doubt that I did love him. He was like my alter ego. When we had discovered we were family I had been astonished, then thrilled and overjoyed in turn. I did not doubt that living together like this was the natural course of things.

But was that as brother and sister?

At some point I started to ask myself the question that I'd never put into words before.

Then came a night when Chihiro was away on a business trip. I was home having dinner by myself and remember thinking that it was awfully quiet. For some reason I didn't feel like turning on the television and instead sat at the table staring into space.

The house felt empty. Chihiro's room was empty. The apartment was utterly silent.

Did I really love Chihiro as a brother?

The thought that I'd never squarely confronted before floated into my mind all of a sudden.

I was in a calm, tranquil mood. When I heard the question in my own voice, I sensed that now was the time to think about it. And so that's what I did.

I sat at the kitchen table, not stirring an inch, and thought about it all night.

Before I knew it, sunshine came slanting through the gap in the curtains. I slumped to the table with a groan, knocking my forehead against it over and over as I felt myself sinking deeper into a dark pool of despair.

*

No, you're not. Yuji's voice.

No, we're not. My voice.

No, we're not, we're different. Chihiro's and my voice in unison.

On that rainy Friday night, Yuji had calmly looked me in the face and announced, "I've been notified."

It was getting close to the period for transfers in the company, and I knew that the chances of him being transferred were high.

"I'm being sent to Hakata. I'd like you to come. Leave that apartment and come with me to Hakata."

It sounded like a final warning.

When he told me this, he looked me in the eye and said it in a voice that sounded like he was giving bad news. As if he was giving me notice.

An icy silence fell between us.

If any stranger had been observing us, they would never have concluded that a marriage proposal had just been made. It was more like a separation announcement.

I started crying.

I didn't realize it until I saw the bartender looking concerned. Yuji gently wiped my face.

At the time I didn't understand why I was crying, but now I do. I had now lost two people I loved.

Yuji's proposal meant that I would be leaving him, and losing Chihiro.

11

Feeling suffocated, I stand up to open the rain shutters and sit on the windowsill. The fact that looking her in the eye is getting harder might also have something to do with it.

I've resisted the urge to smoke so far, but I pull one out now and light up in a hurry. At last, I breathe a sigh mixed with smoke out of the window.

The night is heavy, with cool air rising off the dense summer leaves of the trees in the park. Empty benches glow spooky white under the street lights, and the clock is like a pale face floating in the dark. The warm humid wind does nothing to cool my burning cheeks.

I know it's pointless at this stage rehashing the hell we've been through one more time, but seeing her like this – not even capable of giving me a simple smile any more – kills me. It punches home the enormity of my loss.

Hiro, you're the…

The words she choked back that night were mine too. The wedge they put between us can't be removed now. Ultimately, neither of us finished the sentence aloud, but the pain of it still throbs, deep down.

*

I sat across from her at the kitchen table watching her quietly cry, and feeling like an idiot as the rain poured down outside.

I'll be honest, though. At the time, it felt like victory. I understood then how jealous I'd been of Yuji Takashiro. So her choosing me over him felt like the biggest win of my life. Which doesn't mean I didn't also feel guilty and unnerved.

But as I listened to the rain and watched her shaking shoulders, I was drowning in happiness. A deep, fist-pumping kind that was also a hair's breadth away from panic.

I also had a bad feeling about it all. I knew any happiness we'd had would sour after this. That's why I wanted to get drunk on it for at least one night. I wanted to burn into my retinas the sight of her squirming in pain over me.

When dawn came, the rain eased and we each went to our own room to sleep. Even then I was still basking in idiotic joy.

Later that morning when I woke up and got ready for the day, I was still okay. But then I saw her getting breakfast and the afterglow evaporated in a flash. She would not look me in the eye. I could see that every pore in her body screamed regret and embarrassment. Her rejection was like having a bucket of cold water dumped on me. By the time I walked out of the door I was highly agitated and very glad of an excuse to be out of the house that day. It just so happened I had to go to work, even though it was Saturday.

Only after putting some distance between myself and the apartment did cold reality sink in. With sudden clarity I saw the position we had put ourselves in and the cage we had built for ourselves. It was devastating, and I was horrified by the cruelty of it. I was living with the person I loved. A woman who was waiting at home. Yet that was the very reason it couldn't be home any more.

I was still in a daze when I arrived at the office and got down to work on the urgent data-processing job my colleagues and I had been called in for. The room was silent and the atmosphere dreary. Normally I only work weekdays, and it felt unnatural to be there on a weekend when I would usually be spending my time outside those walls.

My hands moved automatically while my mind was elsewhere. Over and over I saw the sight of her that morning when I had left the apartment as if escaping. I became more and more upset by it. In the afternoon I had a late lunch at a ground-floor cafe in the office building. The crowd was a different one to weekdays, and I felt blanketed by a sense of unreality. I don't know why, but even now I can remember that scene as if I were outside of it. I see myself sitting frozen at the highly polished counter in the high-ceilinged cafe in front of an empty cup, surrounded by a lively crowd of families, groups of young women, and older people from outside the city, all in Tokyo to meet old friends. My seat is the only one with no sound; I am in a vacuum surrounded by an invisible wall that blocks the surrounding hubbub from reaching me. It was like being in a silent movie. The only places that seemed to exist were the cafe where I sat and the apartment where she was.

How were we supposed to go on living together when I went back?

All the joy of the previous evening's victory was gone and had rapidly been replaced by fear. I felt like I was sinking into quicksand, knowing I would become completely submerged but unable to move. I couldn't speak.

That was the first time I resented her. If it hadn't been for that one thing she'd said, we could've gone on as if nothing had happened. I knew I was selfish, but I couldn't help feeling it was all her fault. Not mine. She was the one who'd wrecked the balance we had.

The time to leave the office was getting closer, and that was a problem for me. In two or three hours, when I finished work, there would be no reason to stay in the office cafe any longer. I felt dread in my stomach at the thought. I'd have to return to the cage. Sure, I had created that cage myself, even wished for it, but I knew now I'd never be able to relax there. The thought of two long nights over the weekend seemed like an eternity.

I stumbled out of the cafe into the bright outside world. I felt dizzy.

"Hello?"

A light cheery voice, free and unconstrained, brushed over me like a fresh summer breeze. Who was talking? Then I realized that without thinking I had phoned Misako.

I sometimes still think about what might have happened if Misako hadn't also been working in the city centre that day. About what my fate might have been otherwise. But she was, and she answered my call, and she readily agreed to my dinner invitation. Saved, I thought. Her undemanding company and the safety zone of the scholarly world she lived in was just what I wanted at the time. So I made my escape to Misako, my place of refuge. But inside, my true state continued to be the one I'd been in as I sat at the counter in the cafe.

That's how I still am, frozen, unable to hear or move, and in the grip of dread.

"Sometimes I think that clock looks like a person."

I turn around with a start at the sound of her voice. She sits with her arms around her knees, like a child.

"If I'm ever feeling guilty or worried about something and happen to look at that clock outside, its face makes me feel like I'm being spied on. When I'm alone it can give me quite a fright."

Are you okay? the round clock face on the pole in the park seems to call from the darkness.

"Me too," I say, nodding as I tap the ash from my cigarette. Sometimes the clock face looming among the trees feels like a kindly guardian, at others like a strict warden. An idea comes to me. "Of course – the clock."

"What?" It is her turn to be startled.

"The song he was talking about."

Excitement flows through me as memories come rushing in.

The sun was intense. The sky was clear, stretching on forever like there were no such things as clouds in the world.

We were having a rest break, escaping from the sun to drink water under the shade of the trees. Perspiration rose off our bodies to mix with the smell of grass and make us feel like we, too, were part of the forest.

Our guide was standing a short distance off looking relaxed, when suddenly he turned to us and said, "You two said you met at the university tennis club, didn't you?" as if he'd just remembered.

Then his phone rang and I was struck by the ringtone. It was "My Grandfather's Clock", which had recently become a hit after a popular young male singer had done a cover version.

"Sorry, will you excuse me a moment," he said hurriedly, then quickly walked off and whispered into the phone. After speaking for a while he came back and said, "Sorry about that. Work calling."

"No problem," I reassured him. Then I asked about the ringtone.

He looked a bit embarrassed. "My kid likes it. He can't talk much yet, but he still tries to sing along with me whenever it plays. Never thought a song like this would be a hit. I happened to see it on the ringtone menu, so I chose it."

Aki joined in the conversation. "How adorable. He must have a good ear. I wonder what he likes about that one to make him choose it from all the songs he must hear."

"I guess a slow song like that is easier for a child to hear than contemporary songs with fast tempos and complex beats."

I made noises of agreement then casually said, "Come to think of it, there was a big wall clock at home. An old clock that really did look like it could've been Grandfather's clock. But it broke down when I was a kid and was just for show after that, like in the song. The design was kind

91

of interesting though. It had Japanese and Western-style carvings, like you see in the Toshogu Shrine at Nikko. I used to look at it every day."

"Wow, that'd be an antique now, wouldn't it." He seemed interested.

"Yeah. It was big too, like old clocks are."

His gaze seemed to wander off. "It sounds like a most unusual clock," he said.

This memory comes as a shock. I could kick myself now I see my mistake.

"Was that what did it?"

"What?" She unclasps her knees and slumps over.

"The wall clock. How could I have been such an idiot? Blabbing on to him about the clock in the house where Mum grew up."

The shock is too much, and I leave the window to sit in front of her again. My face must be pale. She looks worried. A brief painful reminder of how things used to be between us.

"The clock…" Her eyes wander.

It's annoying that she doesn't appear to share my shock. How can she ignore such a major slip-up?

"Don't you remember?" I respond in irritated rapid-fire. "The big wall clock in the corner of the passage-way? Although it might have been broken, it was still a decent-looking antique. The paint was peeling, but it was colourful, with that fancy carving at the top. That's right – I even said it looked like the Toshogu Shrine at Nikko. He must've seen it when he went to visit Mum's home. So when I mentioned it, he realized that the clock he'd seen and the one I was talking about were similar."

It'd have to have been a rare clock to be that similar. What an idiot I was. That must have been when he got his confirmation.

"I messed up. And I was trying to be so careful."

She is staring at me blankly while I beat myself up. Almost like she doesn't know what I'm talking about. How can she not see how serious that conversation was?

But the look of scepticism on her face doesn't budge. "The wall clock, you say?" She seems confused. Her voice is hoarse and sounds strange. Chiaki slowly shakes her head. "I have no memory whatsoever of anything like that from my childhood."

12

Thinking back, I've felt uncertain about the past for a very long time. Since, let me see, possibly the very beginning. Every time he talked about his childhood I was uncomfortable. I felt an anxiety, like needles pricking at parts of my own body, that I could not name. For a long time I stifled my feelings.

There's nothing strange about not remembering much from early childhood. That was what I told myself every time I heard him talk about me when I was little, but I still couldn't understand it. I just couldn't see how it was me he was talking about. That's what the honest side of me thought. Could the things he said about me actually be about someone else? The thought did occur to me quite often.

Or perhaps I simply didn't remember. Since I was adopted, I had no way of confirming it with my parents, however, so I kept my thoughts to myself whenever he spoke of such things.

I do have vague recollections of another child in the house. A child that cried a lot, and I remember being cross about it. But I can't say with any confidence if it was a boy or a girl, let alone really him or not.

He, on the other hand, always spoke so confidently that I was embarrassed and annoyed with myself for not being able to remember anything, so I simply went along with whatever he said, hoping to convince myself it was him.

I also have absolutely no recollection of the shoes he often mentions, the ones that apparently squeaked when I walked. If they were as loud as he says, I feel sure that I would have *some* memory of them, but I don't.

When the subject of the wall clock came up just now, I couldn't hold back the niggling unease and I exploded. I expect it's because I was feeling less forgiving now we won't be living together and I won't have to put up with it any more.

"You don't remember? The wall clock?" He looks at me as if I've betrayed him. But I can recognize the guilt in his expression too.

I shake my head emphatically. "No, not in the slightest."

"Even something that unique?"

"I don't remember a thing about it," I say, shaking my head slowly. "If I'm being honest, I hardly remember anything from childhood. You always seemed to remember everything so clearly that I was embarrassed to say otherwise, so I kept agreeing with you, but the truth is that I don't remember anything."

He stares at me after this revelation, as if trying to decide whether I am telling the truth or not.

"Maybe it's because you were adopted out. You probably tried so hard to adjust to your new home that in the process you unconsciously made yourself forget everything before that." Then he adds, like an excuse, "Or maybe you had to take in so much new stuff that all your previous memories were driven out."

Where is this guilt coming from? "That might be it."

"So, we don't share the same memories," he mutters. He sounds sad. I feel awful, but I don't know what else I can do. He lights another cigarette. "In any case, there's no doubt he picked up on that and took it as a clue. Ultimately, I screwed up."

"I don't know…"

There is an awkward silence, different in quality to all the other awkward silences. This one feels brutal.

A mood of desperation overwhelms me. So we never shared anything. It was always hopeless. The things we thought we had shared were an illusion. And now – what are we doing here, now? We should have just left this place and been done with it, but instead here we are in the empty apartment, rehashing painful memories and going on endlessly – about what? When it was all a waste of time and a waste of our lives.

I stare blankly at the wall, and an image of the man flashes across my eyes. I see his broad, powerful back from behind, almost like a projection. Shadows filtered through the trees play across his body as he walks ahead of me at an unhurried pace, along the mountain trail cocooned by lush green forest.

What was going through his head during the time we were with him, when the children he had never seen before, whose existence he had not even known about, suddenly appeared on the scene? He must have been blindsided. What kind of emotion had he experienced as he realized?

"I wonder if he felt under attack by us?" The words slip out.

"What?" Hiro lifts his head.

"When he realized that we were his children, he might have thought we had come in search of our roots and to accuse him."

His face is expressionless. He gives a slight nod. "He might have."

"What would have happened if the trip had gone on?" I say, looking at him.

He looks mystified. "Who knows?"

"I wonder if we would have levelled with him? About being his children."

"I don't think we'd have done that," he immediately declares, and looks at me with a hint of reproach. "At least, I didn't want to reveal myself to him."

I smile bitterly. "Of course. I was the same too. But I wonder about him. When we said goodbye he might have said, 'Do you two know something, by any chance?' or something like that."

He thinks about this, taps the ash from his cigarette, then slowly shakes his head. "He wouldn't have asked. If it was me, I don't think I'd ask. I'd keep up the guide-and-client act to the end."

"I wonder about that."

I picture a scene that will never happen. He sees it too, I expect. The three of us cheering as we emerge back into the glare of asphalt on the road at the base of the mountain. Him and me, standing side by side, turning to acknowledge our guide upon completing the trek. The guide looks at us and smiles gently.

How would he see us? As a guide? As a father? Would he regard us with an attitude of mistrust, indecision or remorse? Perhaps he would have been regretful.

Hiro is coolly analysing that expression while pretending not to notice anything as he thanks the guide: *Thank you for looking after us. We had a wonderful time.*

Would Hiro try and shake the guide's hand? No, he probably wouldn't do that. Standing beside Hiro, I bow, then look at the guide and smile to show my appreciation.

That's all. That's all we would say, and after that we would never see that man again. That was how it was supposed to be. We would wave goodbye and go our separate ways: us back to the hotel for a soak in the hot spring and then on with our lives, and him back to his wife and child.

But that's not how it played out. Instead, the man's life was cut short that day, right before our eyes. What on earth happened in those last few minutes of his life, in that final moment?

The trekking tour was almost over and we were in a melancholy, end-of-holiday mood that day. It was supposed to be our last rest break on the final day and it was gone three in the afternoon, a time of day when we took things easy. With our trip almost over, we were wrapped in the silence of satisfying weariness.

Our resting spot was a small grassy clearing sheltered by broad-leafed trees, with a magnificent view. The itinerary that day had not been too arduous, so we still had energy in reserve.

It was a peaceful afternoon. None of us was inclined to break the atmosphere with chatter and we each moved apart, sunk in our own thoughts. Not because we wanted to be alone: it was simply the flow of things. Anyone who slipped away into the surrounding wall of trees would have been completely concealed from sight.

I was on my own and not thinking about anything much. The scenery filled me with such deep contentment that my brain could not register any more information, though my eyes could see what was before me. There were many things I wanted to think about, ought to think about, but my brain was rejecting the work of thinking. And so it was in this state of emptiness and satisfaction that I found myself crouching down in the grass without realizing it.

Was I sitting, or squatting?

I gazed at the slightly hazy view without really seeing it, while my hands moved automatically, apparently toying with the grass. I know that because I remember the scent of torn grass rising up from around my knees.

I couldn't see Hiro, or the guide. I didn't know where they were.

It's coming back now. This is the first time I have attempted to try and properly recall what happened that day. Something cold begins seeping from my body, little by little.

I have avoided raking over memories of the day all this time, because the thud of something falling, Hiro's pale face and the shock of finding the guide's body at the bottom of a cliff were all things I wanted to forget.

But there is something else. The truth is, I cannot remember much of what happened. I know my mind was somewhere else at the time, but I don't recollect what I was doing then, or what I was thinking about.

It's the same as it is with memories of early childhood – living in the same house as Hiro, the shoes that squeaked when I walked, the wall clock with the special design. I cannot recall what happened at the time that man died. I'm afraid to admit that to myself.

Which raises the question: what am I afraid of? What is it that frightens me? I was simply crouching in the grass the whole time, not moving around, wasn't I? I didn't see anybody, or come across the guide, who was at the least walking around in the vicinity. Why can't I shake off this fear that I did some awful, irrevocable thing? I pose these questions to myself in trepidation, but find no answers.

"Where were you at the time?" I put the question to Hiro. I know that this is simply running away from myself. But his response startles me. He shoots me a cold, tight look of fear. I have an awful feeling that he is going to say something unpalatable.

"I was in the forest, having a smoke." He brings the words out slowly. Slower than he normally talks, as if he is thinking as he speaks. "I had been craving one all day and couldn't hold out any more. But I promised you I wouldn't smoke on the trip, so I was embarrassed and hid in the forest."

"So that's what you were up to." I am relieved. Shrugging off his confession lightly, I give a slight smile.

"I saw you, though. Through the branches, doing something." He stares at me coldly as I blink in surprise. "You were tying bits of grass together."

"What?"

"You were in the long grass at the edge of the cliff, tying up the stalks. I saw you do it, moving a little bit at a time."

"I did that?"

The scent of grass is in my nose again. I feel the uncomfortable sensation of grass tearing in my fingertips. My vision is misted over. Surely not? Surely I didn't…

The scent of grass grows stronger. A close, stifling smell that wafts up from my feet.

13

Finally I've come out with it. I feel kind of strange: relieved and regretful at the same time.

I was suddenly reminded of somebody I used to know. Who was it? A high school friend maybe, or someone in the tennis club at uni. Anyway, this guy was going out with a girl he was crazy about, but she broke it off after a while. And her reason was this: *To tell the truth, I don't like curry all that much.*

That was more of a shock to him than being dumped. You see, curry was this guy's favourite food, especially the extra-spicy stuff, and it was his thing to go around and check out all the curry restaurants. When he started going out with the girl, he thought they'd hit it off because she said she loved curry too, so he took her to curry restaurants on all their dates. But when they broke up, well, he was left wondering why she'd said it in the first place.

I sort of understand the girl's feelings, though, and why she said she loved curry too. They'd just started going out, and she wanted to please him. It's natural to want to show somebody you have the same likes and interests as them. Everybody does it, more or less.

I'm probably remembering this now because of what Aki just said. Because of the childhood memories I thought we had in common. I feel stupid now I've discovered that what I thought were tiny points of connection were only her paying lip service to the past.

How can she not remember something as distinctive as that clock? I don't understand. I know from living with her she has a good memory. I'm not so bad myself, but she really does have an excellent visual memory. And yet she doesn't remember the clock. It's like this woman in the room with me is a stranger suddenly. All that time we were living together was based on false memories.

But that can't be. It can't be.

A terrifying suspicion starts to raise its ugly head inside me.

Was it possible by some chance that we made a serious error? I desperately want to deny it, but what *did* happen the day that man made his exit?

Thinking back on it now, she was acting weird that day. Maybe because we were getting a bit sentimental with the trip coming to an end.

We hadn't been talking, even before stopping for a rest. It would have been some time since I'd probably blown our cover to him, but I was unaware of that as the three of us walked in silence. He, on the other hand, must have been desperately trying to process the information. So during that time all three of us had our minds elsewhere.

I was in a daze too. Tired of thinking about Misako by then, I walked along with my mind empty, just putting down one foot after the other. I was feeling good, pleasantly tired and free and relaxed.

"Shall we take a break?" the guide suggested.

Aki and I both looked at him in surprise. Why did we react that way, I wonder now?

I give it some thought.

She is silent, too, apparently deep in her own thoughts. Time is passing with frustrating slowness while the silence between us grows.

In irritation I tap cigarette ash into a can on the suitcase. I've given up trying not to smoke in here – I don't feel capable of caring about the apartment any more, or about what she thinks.

Then I remember. That's why. We'd only had a break half an hour before that when the guide said this.

The trail that day was not too demanding and we were fine with taking a break once an hour, but the guide was proposing to rest again after only thirty minutes. That's why she and I looked at each other.

"There's a great spot nearby."

That's what he said. We assumed it meant there wasn't anywhere suitable to rest further on, so that's why we were stopping early. Even so, was it my imagination, or did his announcement seem a bit too abrupt, too much like an excuse?

But it was true about it being a good spot for a rest. It was a small, relatively flat glade, surrounded by forest on three sides, with a magnificent view overlooking a cliff at one end. The only thing was that it was a little way off the trail.

We followed the guide as he abruptly turned off the path and strode up a grassy slope. He seemed in a bit of a hurry. Like he suddenly remembered having to be somewhere to meet somebody.

"What a lovely view," Aki and I said, obligingly agreeing.

We didn't have any real objection to stopping there, seeing as how it was such great weather and the view was amazing. But I can't deny having a feeling something was off.

The guide soon disappeared, leaving us to take in the view.

When I saw Aki wander off too, I thought this was my chance. I'd been craving a cigarette the whole time. The day before, I'd managed to hold out – probably because it was a harder walk and I didn't have any breath left to smoke – and planned on doing the same today until we got back to our lodgings, but I was more relaxed, and when the idea of a smoke entered my head I couldn't stop thinking about it. So I sneaked away from her and went into the forest. It wasn't that thick in there, though enough to give cover.

It was nice in the shade, and I stopped sweating. I didn't feel guilty, and I was laughing to myself as I took out a cigarette. I must have had a premonition that I would break my promise about smoking, since I'd sneaked them into my backpack earlier. I have to say, that cigarette on the sly was worth it. I felt like a high school student again, enjoying a guilty pleasure.

Then I heard her voice. At first I thought the guide must be back, so I looked in her direction, in the belief that she was talking to him. But she wasn't. She was alone, and the guide was nowhere in sight.

She didn't stop talking and I couldn't understand why, so I moved in a bit closer to see. There was no mistake: it was her voice all right. She was squatting at the edge of the cliff, mumbling to herself. She had her back to me so I couldn't hear what she was saying, but her hands didn't stop moving. She was knotting pieces of grass together.

It gave me a jolt when I realized what she was doing. Why on earth would she do that? She seemed much too absorbed in it for it to be just a way of filling in a bit of time out of boredom.

I couldn't understand what I was witnessing, and wondered what childish game she was up to. But I wanted to get back to the forest to continue smoking, and soon lost interest.

After I'd satisfied my craving, I headed straight back to the trail. I thought the plan was for us to meet up there once we'd rested. So I didn't look back in her direction again or see her in the glade. But as I was setting out on a shortcut back through the forest, I caught sight of the guide walking quickly towards the glade, though I don't think he saw me. That confirmed it for me – the rest break was an excuse to leave us so he could go off somewhere for his own purposes.

The guide disappeared into the forest. I took my time going back to the trail, and was doing some stretches when Aki arrived.

She didn't seem any different from before. "We're taking things easy today, it seems," she said, like she was asking me to agree.

"Yeah," I said.

The guide was taking his time coming back. If you ask me now if I heard him fall, I can only say I might have.

"Did you hear a strange sound?" she asked, turning to look at me, but I hadn't.

We waited and waited, but the guide never came. It was peaceful there. The breeze was pleasant. But still he did not come, and we became uneasy. We looked at each other.

"I wonder where he is?"

"Maybe something happened?"

"Perhaps he's still talking on the phone."

"Shall I call him?" I pulled out my phone and pressed the guide's number.

Her eyes were glued on me with the phone pressed to my ear. It rang and rang with no answer. After twenty rings or so I hung up.

"No answer."

"That's strange."

We began to survey our surroundings. Perhaps he'd gone ahead of us. But if something had come up, he surely would have told us before leaving.

That was when I first had a bad feeling. I remembered him hurrying towards the glade. If he hadn't come back after that, I reasoned, he must still be there.

"There's a chance…" I started walking off.

"Chance of what?"

"I saw him before, heading for the glade," I answered, not breaking my stride. She hurried after me.

We went back through the forest to the glade. The view of the mountains was magnificent in the quiet afternoon. But there was nobody there.

I felt deflated. He must have gone off somewhere else. We had to look elsewhere. That's what I was thinking.

But something held me back from moving. To start with I couldn't pin down why.

"What shall we do, Hiro? Do you want to try calling him again?"

I stared at the glade with her anxious voice in my ears. Something was different. Different from before.

Then my eyes stopped on one particular spot, and I gave a start. I saw the grassy area at the edge of the cliff. The place where she'd been crouching earlier, playing with grass. It looked to me like there were further signs of disturbance.

"Hiro?"

She was looking at me. At some point I'd wandered over to the cliff edge without realizing it. I stood on the edge and gingerly looked below.

He was down there.

I felt like I'd seen this scene before. That I'd had a premonition of the man lying sprawled at the distant base of the cliff with his arms and legs flung out. It was a steep ravine down there, with a low river running through it. The man lay sprawled on its bank like a doll on white sand.

He looked so small, I never would have imagined it was the same person we'd been walking with a short time earlier.

"Hiro?" she called, seeing me frozen to the spot, but she didn't attempt to come closer.

"He's down there." It took all I had to say those few words. I heard her gasp. "He fell from here," I muttered, and I began to shake. "He's so far away. Way too far," I murmured.

Our guide was in a far-off place. Much too far ever to be in touch with him again.

Clearly he was already dead.

14

He's so far away. Way too far.

My memory of the time I was alone is fuzzy, but his words still echo in my mind. As well as the abstracted, hopeless note in his voice.

I wouldn't say what came next was a nightmare, more like watching a stream of silent moving images.

He contacted the emergency services and told me to wait there by myself while he went to look for a path down to the bottom of the cliff. My legs wouldn't move – I couldn't even bring myself to peek over the edge.

I don't remember how long I waited. We weren't that far from the base of the mountain, so it can't have been too long. Before I knew it there was a buzz of noise down below. The commotion grew as more people arrived.

Hiro called my phone to say the authorities wanted to talk to us. He was coming to get me and then we would go down with an escort. He arrived with a member of the local fire crew, and we descended the mountain together.

"Too late?" I asked.

"Yeah," Hiro said.

A police officer asked us numerous questions, but as we had only just met the guide it seemed apparent that the locals were not greatly interested in us. We were, to all appearances, simply hikers from the city who they could not imagine being involved in any way with his death.

The police officer and firefighter seemed to know each other, and interspersed the interview with comments such as "Not another one in that place" and "He's got a small kid."

After giving our contact details, we were allowed to go. Though we were prepared for the family to contact us to ask about his last hours, no one ever did. We never heard anything more, not even from the police. We were worried in case it came out that we had been using false names and aroused suspicion, but in the end it seemed that we were simply regarded as outsiders passing through. An article in the local newspaper consisting of a few lines was the last we ever heard of the guide.

He's so far away. Way too far.

His voice comes back to me. In retrospect, it was like a prophecy.

Hiro, the guide, that day and the accident now all seem like nothing more than something that happened a long time ago.

"Did you talk to him at the time, Aki?" Hiro asks.

"At the time?"

"During our last rest break."

"I didn't speak to him," I insist. "Honestly. I was off in a world of my own. I didn't even see him."

It was the truth. I don't know what I was doing, but I do know that I did not see him. Or that's what I desperately tell myself.

"In other words, at the time all three of us went off on our own, quite independently." He stares at the empty can on top of the suitcase, considering this. Tap, tap, tap goes the cigarette on the edge of the can. He is smoking more. A sign that he is concentrating. "What the hell was he doing then?"

"Doing?"

"It came back to me. We had a rest break half an hour before then. But there was something the guide wanted to do, so he manoeuvred us into taking another break. He deliberately took us to that spot, left us there, then went off somewhere and came back. Why on earth would he do that?"

"To go to the toilet – or make a phone call?"

"Yeah, that's what I thought at first," he says, nodding gravely. "But when I think about the way he was acting at the time, I get the feeling he had another purpose."

"Another purpose?"

"It's just a hunch, but maybe he left to check on something."

"Check on something? What could he check up on in a place like that?"

"I don't know. But I have the feeling he went off in a hurry to find out something and didn't want us to see him doing it," Hiro says, lighting another cigarette. He sinks into thought again.

Find out something? What would he want to check up on there? What did he so desperately want to know, in the middle of the wilderness?

"I wonder if... if it had something to do with us?" I venture nervously.

Hiro looks at me without expression. "I think that's a reasonable assumption."

"All right. Let's get this straight," I say, spreading both hands wide.

I'm getting more and more confused as to what is actually under discussion. Is it us, that man, the past or the future?

"The guide saw your knife and realized that you were using a false name. Next, you talk about the wall clock and he becomes suspicious that we – or at least you – are the child of his former wife. Is that what you're saying?"

"Yeah, I guess so," Hiro agrees, then adds, "Yeah, that's right. I was the only one he was suspicious of. It probably never occurred to him that we were both his children."

Only one. The words flash through my mind. Making me pause for some reason. *Only one.* But I cancel the thought and continue. "If that was the case, what do you think he would have done? Up in the mountains, how could he confirm if it was true or not?"

"That is the question." He gives a slow nod, but as I expected, he doesn't appear to have any further idea.

You're up a mountain in the middle of nowhere. How would you go about checking whether the person you are with is your son, without letting on to the other people in your group? Would it even be possible?

We focus our attention on this question. But I am still thrown off balance by Hiro's revelations about the wall clock and me tying the grass, along with my hazy memory.

His words are a profound shock. As if somebody has grabbed me by the shoulders and shaken me roughly, telling me to open my eyes and think hard, because the world is not the place you think it is.

But I do remember some things. Like the way the grass was disturbed in the spot next to the cliff where the guide fell. I feel sure that's where I had been squatting. I may not have seen him, but if I had been tying bits of grass together in that spot, as Hiro says, it means there is a possibility that I killed the guide.

My chest squeezes and my temples go cold. I can see it happening in my mind. The guide walking quickly towards the cliff's edge, stumbling on something and toppling forward.

I can't imagine that he would be caught out by such a simple trick. But then I can't say that he wouldn't either, if there were something to trip him in an unexpected place...

That's why Hiro has been suspicious of me all this time. Fearfully, I examine his face. He is suffering, I can see that. It has been hard for him to carry that burden.

I have to get hold of myself. He must be trying to make me confess. Am I going to be turned in to the police? Am I really a murderer? My head spins.

It has never even occurred to me that I might end up in this position, or that he would doubt me like this. Is he going to give me an answer? Or is it up to me? Will it come out during the course of this night?

I look for something to cling on to, and reach for the bottle of tea. The bottle has been sweating inside the plastic bag and is damp, just like me. I drain a cup of lukewarm tea in one gulp and immediately pour another.

"I'll have one too." He casually holds out his cup and I fill that as well. My eye falls on the cigarette in his fingers, now considerably shorter.

Cigarettes.

It was strange the way the half-smoked cigarette seemed to loom large and fill my vision in that moment.

"Cigarettes."

He looks at me dubiously. I didn't realize that I had spoken out loud.

"You sneaked off to have a cigarette, didn't you?"

He looks startled.

I have an image in my mind, some kind of flashback, along with a visceral memory of the faint smell of cigarette smoke on him when we met up again on the trail. I noted then that he had broken his promise not to smoke during the trip.

A cigarette. A half-smoked cigarette.

"Was that the only time? Did you smoke in the previous rest break too?"

He shakes his head. "No, I didn't."

"Then somewhere else, close by?"

"What do you mean, close by?"

"The man suspected that you might be his son. But he couldn't ask you directly. So what would you do, in his shoes?"

"To find out whether or not a person with you is your own son?"

I nod. "There is a way to do it later, if you can't do it on the spot. Using hair. Or body fluid. If you obtain something like that you can compare it to your own."

"Aha."

Simultaneously, we both look at the cigarette in his hand.

"A cigarette butt would be ideal. Haven't you seen it in movies? With a single butt you can get an accurate confirmation."

"That's true. With DNA testing."

"I'm sure that's what occurred to him while we were walking. If he could obtain a sample from you, he could use it after we had gone, to check if you were his son. You didn't throw anything away between the two rest stops, did you?"

"No, no – oh, hang on." He denies it vigorously at first, then looks uncertain.

"The break before that was at a normal rest spot, wasn't it?"

"Yes. Other hikers were there too. There were benches and a public phone."

"There was an ashtray."

His gaze traces the cigarette in his hand. Marlboro. Always the same brand.

"I remember. I didn't smoke there, but I did throw some butts away." He sounds tense. "I was craving a cigarette all day, and kept touching the packet and the portable ashtray in my pocket every time we took a break." He pats the pocket on his shirt. "There were a few butts in my ashtray, and while I had a free moment, I emptied it at that rest site. Three or four butts."

"He saw you do it."

This must be the source of my hunch – what a relief to find it.

"While we were walking after that, it dawned on him what it could be used for."

I have a feeling that we are getting to the heart of the guide's motive for hurrying back over a section of trail we'd already covered, and my chest tightens.

"You only smoke Marlboros, and you had thrown away several butts at once. If he went back there immediately, there was a good chance he could collect them. Being recent specimens, it was also highly likely that your saliva was still on them. He couldn't resist the temptation to try and get hold of them."

This was a mountain guide. A person who always picked up any bits of litter he came across, so if any cigarette butts were found in his gear, it would have been assumed that they had been thrown away by careless hikers and that he had picked them up to dispose of later.

"That's why he had us wait at that spot, while he rushed back to the last one. With his legs, he could do it easily."

In my mind I can see the guide sprinting back to the rest ground, panting as he stares at the ashtray stand. Then drawing closer, careful not to draw attention to himself, he peeks inside, eyes open wide in expectation and dread.

15

The past has caught up. That's what strikes me while staring at her white face. For the last year, that day has been chasing us, picking up speed and getting closer. Now it's got us.

Her theory makes sense. The guide deliberately manipulated us into taking another rest break to get us out the way so he could go off on his own. I see the whole thing clearly, him running back to pick up those butts once he remembered me throwing them away.

Did he know? A feeling that could be regret rises at the idea. Did the guide suspect that his client from Tokyo, supposedly there for trekking, had in fact gone to check out his father? He might have suspected it, but in the end he couldn't be certain.

"He must have been upset. And on edge too, worried that we would find out what he was doing," she says, muttering to herself. "That's why he ran back to that spot. But we weren't there any more. What did he do then?" She looks at me in alarm. "I think he panicked. Maybe he thought we had followed him. After all, you might be his son."

"It figures." I nod emphatically.

"So in panic he goes looking for us, and then…"

Heavy silence.

"He fell," I finish with a sigh.

"Maybe."

Past putting on any show, we both sink into silence.

Bitterness rises up. Again I see an image of the man, far away, at the bottom of the cliff.

"We killed him, we – no, I did."

She gives me a startled glance.

Ultimately, that's what it comes down to. Obviously our appearance on the scene threw him and he was not in his normal state of mind. If the shock of that caused him to make a mistake he normally wouldn't, then it follows that we killed him.

No, I did. To be accurate, it was my fault.

In a mood for self-punishment, I rearrange my thoughts.

Never in his wildest dreams would it have occurred to him that we were both his children. It was only me he suspected. And if I hadn't raised his suspicions with talk of the knife and the clock, he might still be alive now, happily cuddling his baby.

"It was an accident, you know," she says in a low voice. "After all, he was the one who slipped. He was careless, that's what happened."

I can't tell if she says this for my benefit or hers. But if it was meant in consolation it fails miserably. If anything, her words turn the screw even tighter on the pain I feel at the cruelty of an unlucky slip that deprived a man – our father – and his family of his life.

For a few seconds I can't breathe. I will have to live with this pain forever. Immediately I feel a dark lump of despair, hard as lead, lodged in the back of my throat. I sit there struck dumb. She goes to pour more wine into my glass, but the bottle is empty.

"All gone," she says, and takes the bottle over to the sink, where she rinses it and turns it upside down to drain. She always does this. If a bottle is empty, she can't be satisfied until it's rinsed clean, no matter what it held. "Do you want shochu?" she asks.

I nod weakly. She mixes the drink in silence and places it in front of me. My hand reaches for it automatically and slowly brings the cup to my mouth. A powerful smell of strong spirits shoots up my nose, making me aware again of the despair stuck in my throat.

"Aha, that's what this is." The words slip out unawares, and she looks at me. "I just had a strange idea," I say, and laugh wearily. I can't believe how old and creepy that laugh makes me sound.

"What kind of strange idea?"

"About *Kokoro*."

"What?"

"*Kokoro*, the novel by Natsume Soseki. You've read it, haven't you?"

She looks confused. "Yes, but what's that got to do with anything?"

"There's one part in *Kokoro* that sticks in my mind. In a letter the teacher Sensei writes, he talks about stealing a girl from his good friend when he was young, and how the friend commits suicide."

"Yes…"

My mood lightens with every word. Talking about this is somehow taking off the pressure. I continue. "Sensei is the one who finds him. The moment he realizes his pal has committed suicide, Sensei knows intuitively that he's done something that can't be undone and has effectively killed his friend."

"Ah yes, I remember a scene like that."

"There's one sentence – and I can't remember the exact words – but he feels like he's seen his future projected in a beam of black light. He has a premonition that his friend's death will cast a shadow over his own life forever. That's what I feel now. Like there's a black light over my future. I understand how Sensei feels. I could write a book report on *Kokoro* now, loaded with all the empathy a teacher could want." I laugh self-mockingly and she responds with low-pitched laughter.

"I wondered what you were going to come out with. But I never would have guessed *Kokoro*."

"It's a first for me to discover a useful life lesson in a work of literature."

"I wonder if it *is* useful."

Maybe it's the shock, but our voices are stiff. We laugh hollowly and sound unnaturally bright. Apparently humans can't take being constantly stressed-out.

"Stupid, isn't it. I might have killed my father."

"Oh, come on, Hiro."

If anyone besides her was looking at me now, I know it would seem warped and totally inappropriate, but I can't stop laughing.

"It's okay, you know."

Something in her voice doesn't sound right. I look at her. She stares vacantly out of the window. Her face in profile shows nothing of the tension there's been so far.

In fact, she doesn't look at all like the pale-faced woman who just told me her theory.

"When we leave here tomorrow, we'll forget about it. It'll be okay, humans can forget anything, can't they, no matter how awful?"

Something hits home.

I search her face for signs of criticism but find nothing. So that's how it is. She's not blaming me, right to the end. The lump of despair in my throat turns to guilt. I feel ridden with it.

She chose me over Yuji Takashiro. I took that as my due and it satisfied my ego, but after the sense of victory wore off I began to resent her for it, because I was about to run off to be with someone else.

But for some reason I can't picture Misako's face. The events of a year ago are so fresh and graphic in my head right now that Misako is like a creature from another world. Thinking about Misako makes me feel safe, though, she's my refuge. I feel proper when I'm in her calm, unsullied presence. In all honesty, I couldn't wait to get out of this apartment and was depressed about spending tonight with Aki, even though it was just one night.

And yet.

In a corner of my mind a vague misgiving raises its head. Will I really be able to live a "safe" life with Misako?

I feel a chill. This is something I've never asked myself before.

When my day-to-day life was filled with peril I longed for shelter, but now the danger is past, will I be content to stay on in that shelter? Will it become a chore eventually, painful even? When safety is my norm, will I be able to stand the boredom?

A shudder passes between my shoulder blades. I have a bad feeling – a hunch, you might say – that I am going to hurt Misako in future. The ugly side of me she doesn't know yet will hurt her badly, make her cry, and her life will end up ruined. I can see it all happening, like in *Kokoro*. In an instant I become so convinced of the truth of this revelation it hurts.

"But you know, in a way I'm happy." She turns abruptly and says it quietly, with a smile.

"Huh?"

Am I hearing right? Did she say *happy*? What the heck does *happy* mean, anyway?

She gives a small laugh, with her eyes cast down. "The truth is, I don't know why that man died. But our appearance on the scene surely had something to do with it." Her eyes have a weird spark of ecstasy in them. "We are responsible for his death. We are accomplices who share guilt for the crime. Forever more. That makes me happy in a way. Are you angry? Do you think I'm mad? I wouldn't blame you if you did." She looks me in the eye with a serious expression. "But I'm still happy. It's the kind of terrible secret I could never tell a soul, but I can share it with you."

A thrill goes through me, along with a familiar heady feeling at this revelation, satisfying a base feeling of pride. She still thinks about me.

"Death is truly mysterious." She glances vaguely out of the window again. "Our situation is not quite the same, but it's what you mean about *Kokoro*, isn't it? The suicide of the teacher's friend becomes a lifelong burden on him. We're like that. Our father was only a name until we met him, but now we're bound to him for the rest of our lives, simply because he happened to die in front of us."

She's right.

That final moment is still burned in my head. And the despondency I've felt ever since. These will always be with me. That's very clear.

"What if it were me?" Her voice abruptly drops a register.

Automatically I look her in the eye and freeze. There's a strange light in them that I've never seen before.

"If I died, would you remember me always?"

"What's this?" I attempt to sound angry, but fail miserably. Scared is the only word to describe my voice.

She gives a low, throaty chuckle. "If I died here, now – or maybe before we said goodbye tomorrow morning, or even after that – would you remember me forever? Do I have the power, I wonder, to keep a hold over you forever, Hiro?" She sounds teasing, but there is a serious note underneath.

"Don't be ridiculous."

My hand gropes for the knife, but I can't find it.

16

My taking his knife and slipping it into my pocket has no particular significance. It might have been because I didn't like it lying it around and he didn't seem inclined to put it away any time soon, combined with the vague yearning I had to hold that compact yet delicate instrument in my hand once more.

Mainly, however, it was simply the fact that it belongs to him and has his name engraved on it. Because I wanted a memento. He has the earring that I put in his bag, yet I had nothing for myself. I know how crazy it sounds, but I felt a sense of injustice over this.

Without thinking, I slipped the weapon unobtrusively into the pocket of my cotton skirt before I knew it. It felt alarmingly heavy, and my heart was in my mouth, but I was triumphant.

In our early days together we often gave each other gifts. CDs we liked, books, photographs, travel souvenirs, or cakes and other small delicacies. When people are in the process of becoming intimate they give each other things, all kinds of small, miscellaneous offerings. Every exchange leaves a mark of one's existence in the other's world and gradually widens the scope of it. Thus by degrees we become special to each other. That's how we were supposed to be.

But that's all over for us, and those objects are no longer necessary. Perhaps he finds the reminders of my existence abhorrent now. I very much doubt that he is taking all the shirts, neckties and handkerchiefs I gave him to his new home.

His closet there will be filled with gifts from the new girl. I am sure she has different tastes. Their apartment probably has a simple, muted interior, like a warm, relaxing early-summer breeze. That's the kind of girl he chose. Someone who won't pressure him like I do. Or look at him wretchedly, or torment him. A girl who won't become heavy baggage.

My heart is on the verge of drowning. As if a wave is surging through its depths, churning up dirty spray, while a festering sensation creeps down my spine, giving off foul vapour.

I hate that girl for going to him in a fresh, pristine state. For believing that she alone is always cloaked in beauty. She takes it for granted that defilement is foreign to her. It's something she believes implicitly, and I hate her for it.

What's up? Are you okay? I can just see her asking him this, oh-so-concerned as she greets him at the door, all innocent and doe-eyed – it makes me want to scream.

It's nothing, he will answer with a gentle smile, and he'll stroke her cheek.

I know I'm being ridiculous to allow myself to become so angry over imaginary scenes like this, but I can't stop in spite of being aware of what a fool I'm being. And despite the fact that she knows nothing about Hiro and me. Nothing about the weight of our time together, our ties to each other, our complicated entanglement and despair. Misako knows nothing of all that.

It may be true up to a point that there is no jealousy without love, but this emotion can still strike me without warning, at any time. Stabbing me with such ferocity, I feel crushed by the cruel pain of it.

There is no jealousy without love. However, the simple fact is that this love is not supposed to exist. I take a deep breath, like a sigh. The back of my throat quivers. I have a tendency to hold my breath whenever I'm in the grip of strong emotions.

I must think about something else. I nonchalantly attempt to pour some more shochu into my cup, but my hand shakes.

Yes, that's it – even if things are good with them now, she will eventually come to see that she has nothing in common with him and knows nothing about him. I know that he will never discuss me with her. Because if he does that, it will plunge the two of them into another kind of hell.

Yet secretly I hope he does let something slip.

The landscape of their domestic bliss is dotted with landmines. In the same way I had a revelation that blew everything apart for me when I touched the scarf, tiny cracks in the facade will continue to appear inside her, fuelling her doubts. Is he hiding something, she will ask herself? Is there another side to him I know nothing of, much bigger than I can imagine? Suspicion will creep up on her in unexpected moments, staying her hand as she hangs up a tea towel or waits for a computer to start up.

Him too. How long will he be able to endure that girl's innocence? After all, I *know* about the darkness in him, locked inside the room he hides from others. Ultimately I did not find out what was in there, but I have seen the door to that room.

He sits in front of me with glacier-like coolness.

I found it impossible to endure Yuji's perfection, so Hiro must feel guilt about the existence of that dark room. When he cannot bear it any longer, the guilt will spill out, drop by drop, in the shape of oblique appeals.

At some point Misako will press him for answers and force him to speak. By then, he will be tired of keeping everything inside and use this as an excuse – knowing him, he will blame her – to finally spit out the truth.

These fantasies give me a masochistic pleasure. I imagine the hurt expression on her face and strained one on his. I'm aware that such mean, petty thoughts are only wounding me, yet I can't help but take pleasure in them.

Slowly, by degrees, their life will change. Shadows from the past will come to loom larger over them day by day, as both grow more apprehensive.

That girl is no doubt thinking that she is untouchable. On her way to a career as a researcher with the path laid out before her, she feels protected by the world of academia and believes herself to be insulated from jealousy or suspicion, above the kind of despicable female cruelty that belongs to another world.

I used to think that too. Lovers' quarrels, love triangles, clichéd stories in television dramas, banal gossip repeated ad nauseam on trashy programmes – there was a time when I believed implicitly that it was all laughable, and immaterial to me.

Now, I can only reflect wryly upon my own arrogance. How ignorant I was, a level matched only by the violence of emotions that assail me. Like the relentless lapping of waves on the beach, washing over my feet and grabbing at my ankles as I sink into the sand and tumble, time and time again, the hem of my skirt, which I had thought would always be clean, becoming soaked in sand and seawater.

I am already out at sea. Floating in the water while gazing back at the innocent girl on dry sand who believes that she will never get wet.

It won't be long. Any second now the wave will arrive to wash around her feet and strike terror into her heart. Then she will know. She will understand that a woman's place is in the sea. Where the acts of floundering, drowning and gulping mouthfuls of salty water while struggling to swim against the current are the true essence of our sex.

"Don't make bad jokes," he says curtly, then repeats himself, sounding angry.

"A joke?" I snap. "Do you think I would joke about such things?"

Maybe it is the sharp edge in my voice that silences him briefly, but he collects himself enough to protest: "I won't stand for you going on about losing flesh and blood."

Well, this is a revelation. His voice is weak and I look at him more closely. "Flesh and blood" is a rather feeble way of referring to the father we lost a year ago, when a few short minutes ago he had been referring to that same father in less than respectful terms. He reads the question in my face and slides his eyes away from mine.

"To be honest, Mum's in a bad way."

"What?" My irritation evaporates at this entirely unexpected response. "Since when?"

"She collapsed a month ago and has been in hospital ever since."

I lean closer. "What's wrong with her?"

"Subarachnoid haemorrhage. She had one once before, a very mild case, but it doesn't look good this time."

"Is she conscious?"

"Yeah. But dozing most of the time. She responds if I call her and can speak slowly."

We both fall silent.

"A month ago – why didn't you tell me earlier?" After all, she is my birth mother.

He looks pained and gives a wry smile. "You know why."

I know what he's saying. He has met my parents, but I have never met his. His mother never wanted to meet me, the daughter she abandoned a couple of decades ago. She kept her son and gave her daughter to a stranger. I, too, could understand why she might be ashamed to meet the child who was not the chosen one. I have no desire to hold a grudge against her for this, and my parents had given their blessing to my meeting her; however, I did also think that there was no necessity for us to meet. There's no question of my going to see her at this point just because she is unwell.

I understand this logically and appreciate his quandary. But I'm still not satisfied, and am annoyed with myself for failing to notice that he must have gone to see her in hospital numerous times.

"What's her prognosis?" I ask, pushing away my discontent.

I won't stand for you going on about losing flesh and blood. His voice echoes in my mind. He must have let his true feelings slip. There can't be much hope for her.

"Not good," he answers. "She's had complete bed rest the whole time. They think there's a possibility the slightest movement could cause another major haemorrhage for one thing, and apparently it's in a difficult position, so there's a good chance any operation might trigger one, or worsen her condition. All she can do is keep still, but even doing that she's lost an awful lot of strength."

"Oh my goodness." It is all I can do to say even this much. "Are you managing all right?"

With one thing and another, hospital patients require a lot of outside help from family. I knew his father was conscientious, but I could imagine how he might be struggling.

"Yeah, Dad's doing a good job taking care of her," he says with a small nod. "Besides, Misako looks in occasionally too."

Another stab to the heart. A surge of the resentment that I've been trying to suppress breaks through the dam. I understand. She does not want to see me, even though I am her real daughter. But as his fiancée, that girl will become family. That's why he can ask her to help with his mother.

"Please let me see her," I cry.

He looks at me in surprise.

"Please let me see her. Even briefly. I don't have to say anything. I'll probably never see her again. That's why I'm pleading with you, let me see her, please."

"That…" Lost for words, he shifts his eyes away from me. I register the confusion and indecision in them. But I feel stunned. This indecision tells me how grave his mother's condition is.

I won't stand for you going on about losing flesh and blood.

"Please."

I shift closer, but still he remains silent.

17

When I see the look on her face, I wish I'd kept my mouth shut.

Idiot me. I never meant to tell her about Mum. But I slipped up in a moment of weakness, when I was upset over the idea of my thoughtlessness sending a man to his death.

Mum never intended to meet Aki. It's her way of drawing a line under the past. But she's deeply remorseful about giving up her daughter. She's hard on herself in some ways.

I thought Aki always understood, because she's never mentioned wanting to meet Mum. I guess she's also being considerate of her adoptive parents as well. I mean, what would be the point of meeting her birth mother after all this time, when it would only add to her worries? And say Aki did meet her once – well, people always have preconceived images in their heads… Knowing Aki, she'd stress out over all kinds of unnecessary stuff. Stew over lost time and what she might have had and so on. I've no doubt their *not* meeting is the best shot at peace of mind for both mother and daughter.

I'm a cowardly piece of shit though. When I look at her face, I can't help feeling disgusted with myself.

There's logic in being callous to the end, if that's how you play it, but it also has its weaknesses. I just can't keep things to myself, even though I try hard to hold out, and I eventually end up folding. When there's only a bit further to go, I shove the decisions onto other people and let them take the blame. That's the kind of prick I am.

The fact that this day has come is my fault as well. Secretly I was looking for a way out of this living arrangement, one that wouldn't make me the bad guy. Then she handed me the opportunity. So because I was already on the lookout for a chance, I managed to put it on her. I railroaded her into coughing out the decisive words, then spent the rest of our time together running away.

But it's even more sickening than that, because I know this self-disgust is only a way of creating an alibi for myself. One part of me calculates that that's what I ought to feel, so I make a show of doing it. But it's only relief at being able to justify myself in the eyes of public opinion or strangers.

The real me feels no guilt or self-disgust. I don't feel a thing – that's right, nothing. I think. Deep down, I probably don't even feel guilty about the possibility I might have driven that man to his death – I was just shocked, that's all.

I've already begun to accept that Mum's time is close. If this was her first hospitalization it might have been more of a shock, but because she's collapsed once before I've been able to take it in my stride.

Luckily, my father is handy around the house and can cope with housework. It's not so common for a man of

134

his generation. He can take care of himself while going to and from the hospital to see to Mum, which is a huge help.

Neither of us have spoken about it, but we both dimly accept that this time she won't be going home. I'm sure Mum senses it too. But she never shows her family the slightest anxiety or fear. Her face is thin and she's always half asleep, but sometimes when she's awake and talking, her eyes are so peaceful and calm it's scary.

I asked her if there's anybody she wants to see. It was the kind of conversation you have with a parent when there's little time left. Whenever she's alert, I have to take the opportunity to discuss a number of things I need to discuss with her. She's past the stage of needing reassurances or being urged to rest up.

"Nobody," she instantly replied.

I watched her carefully to see if that was what she really wanted, but she didn't give anything away. "Okay then, I understand," I told her, but I still hesitated. Because there was one name I had to ask her about.

"What about Chiaki?" I said, trying to be casual.

Mum rolled her head slowly from side to side and said flatly, "Don't tell her about this."

I didn't know how much she meant by *about this*. About being in hospital, or not having much time left, or…?

I wanted to ask, but couldn't say anything. Mum's expression didn't change a bit at the mention of Chiaki. She stared at the ceiling a while and then suddenly said, "I did the wrong thing with you two."

This time I understood she was talking about the both of us, but I didn't know what she meant by *the wrong thing*.

"Why? What do you mean, 'wrong thing'?" I tried not to let her see how much I wanted to know, because I had a feeling that if I leaned in and showed too much interest, she'd clam up and never say another word on the subject.

"I never imagined you two would meet up by accident. That girl must be —"

It was bad luck that I'd leaned a little too far forward on the edge of my chair. Her voice was soft and I couldn't hear properly. But that was enough for her. She stopped mid-sentence, looked at me and said, "Don't tell Chiaki. Wait till it's all over."

This time I understood clearly. Once she had left the world, then I could tell Chiaki. "Okay. I'll do as you say," I promised.

That's when Misako arrived. "Hello," she said gently from the door.

Mum and I both nodded in greeting. After Mum went into hospital I told her about Misako, and I took her with me to visit several times. Then Misako began going on her own.

The three of us talked about safe topics, including my future life with Misako. The object was to reassure Mum.

"She's a good girl," Mum murmured when Misako left. But her eyes were cool, as always. Seeing them made me feel guilty and uneasy. I had a feeling she saw through my performance. That she'd read me completely – my insincerity and heartless abandoning of Chiaki to run to Misako, and the unhappiness I would cause Misako in future.

The chime rang to signal the end of visiting hours.

I left the room with conflicting emotions. On the one hand I felt an almost physical compulsion to stay there, while on the other I was fighting the desire to get out of there as fast as possible.

That was three days ago.

"Sorry. It's my fault. I didn't mean to say anything. Mum asked me not to tell you." I know the only way of heading off her stubborn request is to be tame and apologize.

"Oh, I see." She seems at a loss for words, and looks hurt.

"She doesn't want to worry you. You understand."

Aki turns away at this attempt to smooth things over. I know that logically she understands, but she must feel rejected. I certainly regret upsetting her with my careless words.

"But I'll ask her once more. I swear. I'll convince her that you want to see her. Please, give me a little more time. I promise I'll get in contact with you."

This does the trick, and she grudgingly softens. "Okay. Make sure you do contact me."

"I will."

She looks awkward, embarrassed maybe by the strength of her own emotion, and sips her drink. Since I'm the one who caused it, I pour myself another shochu and guiltily join her.

"I guess Mother had a hard time of it when we were born," she murmurs after a while. "It's such a shame, after raising her son to adulthood, seeing him get a job and marry. Now that she can finally relax, it's not fair, is it?"

"No."

Mum has never once said a word of complaint or about dissatisfaction with her lot, but she would have had plenty to butt heads over with her first husband, who was no longer in the world. How did she feel about him?

"I was young at the time so I didn't really understand then, but her family had debts and money troubles. Then there was her younger sister – I've told you about her, Aunt Funahashi, who was always sick and had health problems ever since she was small. That made things difficult too."

"Oh," she murmurs, to show she's listening. Aki's adoptive parents have few relatives, so talking about them is a rare thing for her, and whenever I do it her face goes blank.

"This family hasn't had much luck with men, Mum once said. Aunt Funahashi also lost her first husband and remarried."

"Humph, luck with men…" She sighs loudly and says in an offhand way, "I wonder if I inherited that."

I grin wryly. "Surely not."

"I'm not joking." She shoots me a glare. "The man she remarried, your present father, seems like a good person, and that aunt went on to make a happy home and family. So it's not simply that she has bad luck with men. She also learns from her mistakes. If learning from mistakes is a family trait, then I hope I can too."

What's this, I think, studying her. She doesn't look like she's being ironic, or having a dig at me. She is gazing into the distance. Not seeing me or the apartment but some place far, far away.

I feel irritated by this. Don't I mean anything to her any more? When we leave this place, will she surprise me by being the one who goes with no regrets? I was supposed to be leaving her, but the truth is that she might be the one ditching me.

I picture her in Vietnam. The breeze gently lifts her hair and she appears at ease and refreshed. Her eyes are alert, with the invigorated look of a woman making a new start – I am already in the past.

Suddenly I feel lonely at being left behind.

It's the first time I've felt any uncertainty about my new life with Misako. Will that peaceful, grounded ordinary life be suffocating? Like being imprisoned forever in a cage with invisible bars, entangled in a soft net of kindness and common sense?

"I'll just wash these things. We've eaten and drunk quite a lot." She stands to pick up the empty food trays. Still bent over, she sniffs the air and says, "It stinks in here. I'll turn on the fan."

She's right. Despite leaving the window open, the room reeks of food, alcohol and cigarettes.

Glancing at the clock in the park, I realize that it is eleven already. Tomorrow is almost here. We've only been here a few hours, but it feels like aeons.

I hear the low buzz of the kitchen fan revolving. Though it is a familiar, everyday sound, it sounds extraordinarily loud. As clean air gradually fills the room, it feels like our time here together is fading away. Tomorrow this apartment will become empty, until new inhabitants move in. No longer will our life here together exist.

There is the sound of running water in the kitchen sink, and the clatter of cans and plastic trays being rinsed. Water drains away like the traces of our conversation tonight.

But the sound of running water keeps going. I look over and see her standing stiff and motionless in front of the sink. Something is wrong.

"Aki, are you okay?" I ask, but she does not move. "Aki?" I repeat, louder this time. Still she does not respond.

Only the sounds of the fan and the water echo through the room.

18

Though I hear him calling, his voice sounds so distant. I cannot move. I should turn the tap off, but the shock is overpowering.

I remembered what happened that day.

The mind and memory work in such strange and unexpected ways. Every day I use the kitchen fan. Every day I hear it whirring, morning and night, whenever I cook or boil water. Yet it is as if I am hearing it now for the first time. Maybe it's because the sound is more conspicuous with the room empty of furniture, crockery and other implements.

This buzzing that saws through my brain is overlaid with the memory of a sound I heard that day in the mountains, a year ago.

I was conscious of a noise. There was a large, annoying insect, a drone beetle perhaps or something like it, buzzing around my head. It was sticking close, and would not be shaken no matter how far we walked or how often I tried to shoo it away. I couldn't be sure if there was only one insect or several; in any case, it must have been the odour of my sweat that drew it. The noisy whir of its wings was an irritation, but despite numerous attempts to deter it from flying persistently around my head, I eventually gave up and let it be.

It was our second day of trekking, and tiredness might have been a factor in what happened next. Gradually it began to feel as if I was hearing the buzz in a dream. It repeatedly grew distant and close, and reminded me of the sound of a motor, or a mechanical vibration, or the echo of a tuning fork.

Then something odd happened. Although I was awake and walking in broad daylight, it was as if my mind was in a dream.

The route wasn't as demanding as the day before, and I had been walking on automatic pilot. Distracted, moving along in a somnambulant state induced by a combination of weariness and heat.

I have had this same experience sometimes on the train going home at the end of the day when I am tired from work. I can be standing in a swaying carriage, clutching the overhead strap and looking out at the scenery going by, but seeing something different in my head. My senses become dull, disappear even, as the only thing registering in my consciousness is the rocking of the train and the images in my mind. Dream and reality overlap so that both are visible at the same time. That's what it was like this day.

Until now I had completely forgotten about the day-dream I had then. It was such a curious scene that I didn't know if I was dreaming or delusional.

There were two children playing together. A boy and a girl. They were in a dim grey space, I'm not sure where, but it could have been inside or outdoors. They were crouched on the ground, whispering to each other.

One of the children is me. The boy seems to be Chihiro. Chihiro and I, as children, chatter away together. Our hands move as we talk. We are busy with some task, though I cannot tell what.

The odd thing about this, however, is that although the girl is me, in the dream I can also see myself from the outside. I cannot hear the pair's conversation and move closer, but though I hear their whispered voices I cannot tell what they are saying.

Then a loud, clear voice yells "Hey," and they immediately turn in its direction.

"Let me play," the voice says cheerfully. In the distance I see a shadow waving its hand. Another person, a small girl, runs over to the pair.

The sight of her face gives me a start. The girl is me. She has the same face as mine when I was a child.

I don't understand. If the girl who just arrived is me, then who is playing with Chihiro? She is also supposed to be me, and it does feel that way.

I try to move even closer to the pair crouching on the ground. Chihiro's face is clearly visible since he is facing me, but the girl has her back to me and I cannot see her face.

What's going on? How can both girls be me? What does the me kneeling on the ground look like? I fervently appeal to the small girl's back. I crane my neck, desperately willing her to turn a little so I can get a better look. But she is focused on her hands and gives no sign of turning around.

My frustration builds. Let me see your face. Show me your face, I think.

Then the other me, the one that came later, squats down too and begins to play. The three of them ignore my entreaties and give no sign of noticing me.

What on earth are these children doing? Gradually, my focus shifts to this question. I try to see their hands. They move busily, with purpose. Then the scene moves into close focus, like a camera zooming in. It becomes apparent that they are playing in sand. Each child is scooping it up with both hands and pouring it onto a pile. They appear to be burying something.

What could it be? I focus on their hands. There is a black object. Rather large. What is that black thing?

The grating buzz in my ears continues. Insects fly about me. Are they flying near the children, or near me? I can't tell, but there are many of them.

The children keep piling up sand. Their small hands move tirelessly in a scooping motion, covering the black object with handfuls of gritty grey sand.

"How about we take a rest. There's a good spot nearby," the guide proposed.

Hiro and I looked at each other doubtfully. It hadn't been long since our last rest break, but maybe the guide noticed that I was tired.

The drone beetles, or whatever they were called, were buzzing around my ears. Perhaps they were attracted by the smell of my sweat, but they would not leave me alone.

The children doggedly continue scooping sand. They are determined to cover this thing. Together they will bury that black object.

There was no denying that the rest location suggested by the guide did have a magnificent view. It was a small clearing mostly surrounded by forest near the edge of a cliff, the kind of place that would have been a secret hideaway in childhood.

Three children playing, scooping up sand.

Before I knew it, Hiro and the guide both went off on their own. I was alone, like a child in a secret hideout.

Without thinking, I crouched on the ground, and a warm moist smell of grass rose from beneath my feet. There was a buzzing in my ears.

The warm, suffocating grass smell wrapped itself around me. The buzzing grew louder, merging with the odour, enfolding me.

And then I was back in childhood. On a day long ago, when I was little. How old was I? Was it before or after he and I were separated?

We have to bury it.

I scoop up the sand at my feet with both hands. Small hands move automatically, digging up sand to bury the black thing.

Bzzzz, bzzzzz, bzzzzz.

Something flies around me. Or maybe it is the sound of a motor. My hands carry on moving in a smooth scooping motion, digging up sand to bury the black object.

"Aki! What's wrong? Don't you feel well?"

A voice behind me finally brings me to my senses. I turn and see him standing behind me, staring at me pale-faced.

"Ah? Ahhh." I answer vaguely, and turn off the tap jerkily. I hear buzzing and slowly lift my head. It is the fan, not insect wings, spinning relentlessly.

I wipe the sweat from the back of my neck and switch off the fan. After a short time, the room finally becomes quiet.

"What's up?" he asks again.

I look into his face. The child in my dream digging in the sand has become a pale-faced young man.

A young man I love. Who is now regarding me as if I am repulsive.

"I remembered – the sound of the fan brought it back. To think I've heard it every day... Memory is so strange, isn't it?"

"Remembered what?"

"What happened that day. On our last break."

"What?"

I put the newly washed trays into a plastic bag.

"All this time I haven't been able to remember properly what happened that day – only that it was hot, that I was tired and a bit disorientated. But just now it came back."

"What did you remember?"

I knew he was holding his breath, waiting for me to continue. What did he hope for, I wonder? A confession of murder? Or —

"I wasn't tying up the grass," I answer with a sigh. "I was burying something."

"Burying?"

146

His confused expression irritates me. How can I explain what had happened to me that day?

"I can't explain it well, but at the time, I was remembering when I was little. I don't know if it was something I dreamed, or if it actually happened, but my hands were copying movements I had made as a child. Haven't you ever done that? You wake up from a dream, and before you can tell if you're still in it, you cry out, or speak to people in the dream? Hasn't that ever happened to you?"

"Yes, but…"

I can see that he is bewildered. I don't blame him. I can't explain it myself.

"I saw you and me as children. We were playing with sand, then another girl came along, and we all played together."

"Another girl?"

"Yes. The three of us were digging up sand with both hands and burying something."

I didn't tell him that the other girl was also me. It would only complicate the discussion, which was already hard enough to get my head around. He would only be more confused than ever if I mentioned it.

He makes a scooping motion. He repeats it several times and then falls into thought.

"It's true, now you say it, that what you were doing could look like digging up sand to bury something."

We return to the tatami room and sit facing each other across the suitcase again.

"There was an annoying buzzing sound that day. The insects wouldn't stop flying around my head. It has to be related to something from childhood. Just now, the sound of the fan brought back a memory – just like the sound of insects that day triggered a childhood memory."

My conviction grows stronger with every word. I hear my voice becoming more certain.

Though I can see that he, too, is still dubious, he nods as if satisfied.

It comes to me then. The nature of the black object. The large black thing we were busily covering with sand.

"It was a child," I blurt out.

The three of us had been burying a child.

19

It takes me a while to catch on that something is up with her. When I do, it completely throws me.

The sight of her in this weird state reminds me of when Mum collapsed. That was in the kitchen too. I was sitting at the dining table while she chatted to me from the kitchen, when suddenly she stopped. I looked over and saw her standing there, not moving. I called out a few times but she didn't answer, which was strange, so I got up and went over. Then the second I reached her, she sort of crumpled on the spot, in front of the sink.

This image sticks in my mind, overlapping with the sight of Aki now, so when she goes to switch off the kitchen fan it's a huge relief.

I don't know what was going through her head while she stood there frozen, but I believe her when she says she was thinking about last year.

Once the fan finally stops the room is weirdly quiet. I can hear insects chirping outside, but they seem a long way off.

All things considered though, her story sounds crazy. She started talking without warning about a daydream she had a year ago in the mountains, which you'd have to be out of your mind not to wonder about.

But on the other hand, it does add up.

That thing she was doing with her hands that looked like tying grass – I can see how it could look like burying something. And I can also accept that the blank look on her face at the time was a reaction to waking up from a dream.

What on earth am I supposed to think about three children playing in sand, though?

To hear her talk so feverishly about a dream she had a year ago makes her sound like one of those fake mediums you see on TV. She's usually so calm and collected that it's weird seeing her this way.

"We were burying a child." She looks at me with a pale face.

Those eyes are like black holes. Bottomless, nihilistic holes. They make me feel afraid.

What is she saying? Is she confusing childhood memories with dream and reality? Is she playing with me? Is this supposed to be some kind of punishment?

I inch away from her. I want to run. Get out of this room. Away from her. Away from the past, and away from the future too.

For a moment the impulse is overwhelming.

But where can I run? Where can I go? Into another cage with Misako? I can't think of anywhere. Only a pure white empty space. Where there is nobody and nothing. It's the only landscape filling my brain.

Maybe I should stay here and let myself be sucked into those eyes. The bottomless darkness in there could very well be my own. Maybe it's simply my own nothingness I see reflected in her. If she's willing to go there with me, then maybe we should just let ourselves.

As I begin to falter, life returns to her eyes. "Sorry." She looks around as if to confirm where she is.

"I don't know what to make of your explanation, actually."

She looks disappointed and sighs heavily, then runs her hands impatiently through her hair, mussing it.

I'm tired. It's like an interrogation room in here with that light on the ceiling and suitcase on the floor. But who is interrogating who?

She stretches and shifts position, then pours drinks for both of us.

"Let me explain once more."

Now she's back to her usual cool self, I'm more open to hearing what she has to say. This time her explanation satisfies me. I see how her actions that day could be explained. And that dream of hers raises some interesting points.

"The dream has to be connected to a childhood memory. That's my feeling."

"So who's the third girl then? Do you remember anyone?"

"I don't know. Maybe, maybe not. I don't know her name. You don't remember anyone, do you, Hiro? We might have seen her together."

I give it some hard thought. I remember playing with other kids in the neighbourhood, but don't recall any one particular girl.

"What about the play area with the sand? Was there one near our home?"

"Hmm." I can't think of anything. I do have a few memories of playing in sand, but couldn't say whether they happened at school or in a local park.

Hang on though, didn't we just establish that there are discrepancies in our memories?

"You don't remember much of your early childhood to begin with, Aki, so let me ask you this: what *do* you remember from when we lived in the same house?"

"So, umm…" She seems to be having difficulty. "To be honest, I don't really remember anything. Being in the same room with a boy having a tantrum is about the sum of it."

"Me?"

"Errr… I guess so."

"But you remember playing in the sand with a third child, a girl."

"Yes, I think that happened."

She is stubborn on this point. Her expression tells me she isn't lying. Her instincts are usually right, which means I'm the one who can't remember it.

"A girl. I don't know. There were lots of girls in the neighbourhood."

"What about noises?" she asks.

"Noises?"

"Yes, noises. Like I associated the exhaust fan with the sound of insects flying about. Maybe the sound of insects triggered a childhood memory that day last year. I feel certain that I heard something similar when I was little. Do you remember anything like the fan?"

"Can't say I do. It's all too misty and vague." I look up at the ceiling. "So, what about us burying a kid then? Are you saying that really happened? That we killed somebody and buried them in the sand?"

"I don't know about that." She wrinkles her forehead

in thought. "No, I don't. I think it must be some kind of metaphor."

"Metaphor?"

"Dreams aren't always direct, are they? When you have a dream, you tend to ascribe it to something else that happened, say an argument you had during the day, or an unpleasant experience that's represented by a horrible animal. Don't you have dreams that make you see the reasons for things more easily?"

"I do."

"Right. I think it's something like that. The children in my dream actually existed, but maybe burying one of them in the sand means something different."

"Like maybe there was a snotty kid we wished would disappear? Can you think of anyone who fits the bill? If you disliked someone enough to want to bury them, I'd think you'd remember who they were. So, do you?"

"No. No one springs to mind." She looks annoyed.

This must be frustrating for someone who has a good memory. It's amazing how she managed to drag up that particular scenario after so much time. Strange too, how it was the fan that brought it on, when I can't remember a thing...

We drink shochu in silence for a while.

She seems to be determined to dig through our childhood memories, but personally I feel more and more like I don't give a damn. When all's said and done, it's just a dream. Who knows how much is true? Besides, it's her dream, not mine.

More than that, though, the significance of the fact that she wasn't tying up bits of grass to make a trap or anything is starting to sink in. Which means, essentially, that the responsibility for the man's death rests even more squarely with me.

Going over all this again is depressing. I'm jealous. She's clear of suspicion now. That's why she can concentrate on things like childhood memories.

I don't see any point in stressing over it any more at this stage. Even if nothing had happened that day in the mountains, something else might have happened somewhere else the next day, or maybe a car accident. It's done, there's no point dwelling on it. At least that's what I tell myself, but now I've started thinking about it again I can't stop.

"Hey, Hiro, do you remember the address of where we used to live?" she asks.

"What?" The unexpected question throws me.

"It's the same house where Mother grew up, right? Do you know the address?"

"I can't remember the house number."

"The block name is enough."

I tell her my vague recollection of the address and she thanks me, then sinks back into thought. Mum's address? What is she thinking?

I watch her as she gradually appears to come to a decision. She begins clearing the top of the suitcase.

"What are you doing?"

"Sorry, just moving these things out of the way. I'll put them back soon." She deftly opens the suitcase a fraction and extracts a laptop from inside.

"What do you need that for?"

"Just something." She pulls out a bundle of cables as well and fumbles with the cords to untangle them. Then she crawls over to the phone jack in a corner of the room and plugs it in.

So, she wants to use the internet.

I don't like this somehow. I wanted to be with her alone tonight, away from the outside world. I couldn't care less about that man's death any more. Isn't it enough for her to know it was my fault?

I knew there would be friction tonight, and it's true I wanted to avoid it, but all the same I don't want this last night together interrupted by the phone or computer. My look of displeasure doesn't stop her switching on the computer, though.

"Sorry, I'll be done soon. I hope I can confirm this," she says with her face to the screen.

What am I supposed to make of this? Does it have anything to do with us? I don't see how anything she could find on the internet could be relevant.

I pull out another cigarette and light up. I've already smoked a lot, but I've given up counting because it can't be helped tonight.

The time is one in the morning, already the middle of the night. Through the window I see a sprinkling of lights still on. Japanese people are real night owls these days.

The clicking of the keyboard fills the room. You wouldn't have heard this noise in any home twenty years ago. It sounds so cold and impersonal. Maybe she doesn't have anything to say to me any more. The same sound probably fills many homes today, homes without conversation.

The night drags on. But dawn comes early in summer. By the time we lie down to get some rest, it'll start getting light before we know it. Then we'll get up, rub our eyes blearily in the morning light, and wait in a daze for the tradesmen to arrive.

My mouth tastes acrid. I wash down more shochu and drift into space. Then suddenly I realize something is going on with the clicking of keys.

She always types without hesitation or error, but the sound her fingers make now is random and unpredictable. Her touch is rough and the rhythm erratic.

Eventually, after one particularly violent clacking, the keys go quiet. She must be waiting for the screen to appear after pressing Enter.

"What does this mean?" she gasps.

20

I stare at the screen, not knowing how to interpret the facts on display. What do they *mean*? Can this really be the case?

The atmosphere in the room instantly changes with the abrupt intrusion of reality into the night thick with suspicion, which had until now belonged to us alone.

Reality. The very word has a strange ring.

I was under the impression that tonight, our last night together, was reality, but all along we have been surrounded by another powerful and more impersonal reality. In the face of the hard, uncompromising nature of it, I am too stunned to react.

The site I opened was that of the local newspaper where our birth mother grew up. I wasn't expecting to find anything specific there. The dream with two versions of myself in it had bothered me, and I simply opened up the computer out of vague uncertainty. My fingers reacted before my brain did, seeming to move by themselves, searching.

Since the children in my daydream had been between two and four years old, I searched for articles from when I would have been about that age.

Burying a child in sand had to be a symbol of something.

Something our memories had suppressed. At least that was my instinct. Then that article caught my eye.

"What?" he asks uneasily, drawing closer. He does not look pleased.

"What do you make of this?" I gesture at the screen.

Girl Falls into Construction Site Pit

At 7 a.m. on the 20th, workers arriving at the site of an apartment block construction site at 1 Sakae-machi discovered the body of a small child in the foundations of the building. Her death is believed to be accidental, caused by falling into the pit.

The girl's name was Miyuki Takahashi, aged three. She had been playing in a park the previous day with other children when she disappeared, and a search request had been filed. The site was fenced off and enclosed with tarpaulins, but she was apparently able to enter through a gap.

"Miyuki Takahashi —" He stares at the article.

"Do you think it's relevant? The address is nearby, isn't it? In the same Sakae-machi, block one."

My foreboding grows stronger. I could be completely off the mark, but my instincts say otherwise. This is it, I feel sure.

He says nothing. Apparently he is trying to gather his thoughts.

I press again. "The surname is Takahashi too – pure coincidence, do you think?"

"No, it might…" His face turns grave as tension rises in him. "What year was this?"

After checking the date of the article he pulls away from the computer and sits down heavily, clasping both knees and lost in thought as he searches through his memory.

I continue to scan the site, looking for follow-up articles, but find nothing. This was the beginning and end of the story as far as the newspaper was concerned. I shut down the computer and pull the cord from the plug. The screen goes black. It's a relief to shut off the internet and leave that menacing reality to retreat back into our own private world. This apartment, which had felt so stifling before, suddenly feels strangely like a haven.

"Maybe – no, it has to be…" He scratches his face. I can tell he's rattled. The unflappable Hiro is losing his cool. This only fuels my edginess further. Why the thumping in my chest? He shoots me a look. Those eyes tell me he is just as shaken as I am.

"There's nothing to corroborate it, but…" He licks his lips nervously. "I think it's my aunt's daughter."

"What?" His reply stuns me.

"Remember Aunt Funahashi, who I mentioned earlier?"

"You're saying it's our aunt's child? Our cousin, in other words?"

"Yeah." He nods. "I'm pretty sure there was a period after Mum divorced when she reverted to her maiden name and went back to live with her parents. And that was around the same time my aunt also took her maiden name again after her husband died."

"So our aunt went back to live with her parents too?"

"No. She wasn't well, I heard, and went somewhere to convalesce."

We search each other's face, both awkward and uncomfortable. Something is making us both uneasy. I can't say what, but it is growing stronger.

"Mum did briefly once mention that her sister lost a child. She didn't say so in as many words. But I remember thinking that's what happened. I knew she wasn't strong, so I assumed it was a stillbirth." His words roll out slowly. "But I bet this Miyuki Takahashi is that child."

"It was an accident, wasn't it?" I say.

We fumble with our glasses to pour more drink, and take a sip. This gnawing unease in the pit of my stomach is not going away.

"I wonder if we ever played together? She would have been around our age, and if Aunty ever visited her parents then it's possible."

"Yeah, it's possible," he agrees, speaking in a low tone.

"Do you think that's what my dream was pointing to?" I had to ask. Though I knew he couldn't answer because it was, after all, my dream.

"Maybe." He's hedging. His voice is hard.

"Yes, we could have played together, and I remembered her disappearance in my dream." I know how lame this sounds. We are both well aware that the problem is not solved. Why would I have remembered the accidental death of a cousin more than twenty years earlier, in the mountains on that day? Why, after all this time, would I remember something I had never once recalled before? Clearly, he wonders too.

"It was a girl child, wasn't it?"

At the age of three, Miyuki Takahashi would have been at her cutest. But that is also an age when a child can wander off in the blink of an eye. That's what led to her crawling through a hole in the fence and meeting with an accident.

"Did Aunty have any more children?"

"She remarried and had two boys. The elder is in high school and the younger in primary school."

"Oh, I see." I sip on my drink and think about the girl who would have been around my age now if she had lived. The difference between life and death can be a single fateful moment. How awful it must be for a mother to lose a child.

"I wonder why you had that dream then?" He looks at me reflectively, swilling the drink around in his cup. It's not surprising he is wondering this as well.

"That is the question," I agree, tilting my head to one side. "Perhaps I couldn't help thinking about the past because we were with our father that day. Childhood memories, buried in my subconscious, started coming to the surface."

"I guess so." Despite this answer, the expression on his face – and probably mine as well – indicates that he is still not convinced.

Miyuki Takahashi… Somewhere there has to be a point of connection with her. I wonder what she looked like.

Two children playing in sand. Chihiro and me. The girl has her back to me. Another girl runs over to them.

A question rises in my mind. Could it have been Miyuki Takahashi?

"Listen, you said Aunt Takahashi was convalescing somewhere, didn't you?"

"Yeah."

"So who was looking after Miyuki?"

"Umm…" He looks thoughtful. After a few seconds his eyes open wide, as if something has occurred to him. "That's it – she stayed with one of the neighbours. A lady who used to work in a nursery and was qualified in childcare. She often looked after local kids at her home apparently. It was an enormous help."

The more he speaks the stronger his memory appears to grow, and the words flow more easily.

"Yes, now I remember – she was a really nice old lady. Come to think of it, I think I went there once too. No idea why I would have been sent there, but I do remember it now. And yes, it was over a dry-cleaner's and boiling hot in summer."

My body stiffens. Why? A chill has run down my spine in response to something he just said. What on earth could it be? Which particular part?

Try as I might, the words slip from my mind before I can grasp them. The skin on my face is taut with frustration. He is still talking to himself.

"I wonder if that kind of place was officially registered as childcare? Nowadays everyone's so conscious about who's in charge in case anything happens that it must be a lot harder to find babysitters for children. But she was a really nice old lady."

Registered childcare centre. Old lady. Babysitter. I examine my reaction to these words.

No, that's not it. It was something else he said about the children. Something before that —

A dry-cleaner's. Boiling hot…

A loud buzzing reverberates in my brain. Next moment, something clicks into place.

Bzzzzz, bzzzzz, the drone beetles circle my head. Sticking to me persistently no matter how much I brush them away. Their grating buzz saws through my mind, becoming distant and close by turns.

Electric fan. The words flare in my head and I hear the whir of an electric fan in a room above a dry-cleaner's, on a blazing-hot summer's day.

Then in a flash I see it. The daydream. In it, Chihiro and I are playing in the sand, but my back is turned so I can't see my own face. Then another girl runs over. A girl with a face I know. Me. That girl too is me. In other words, this scene means —

"Hiro."

"Yeah?" He looks at me.

"I think I know what happened."

"What happened where?"

A bitter taste fills my mouth. It can't be, not now. Why now? Can it really be possible? But this is what all the facts point to. I can't believe it... Surely not?

Though conscious of his gaze urging me to explain, I still cannot speak.

21

Facts and the truth. What do they mean anyway? What value do they have?

I've been giving this a lot of thought lately.

In movies and TV dramas you always see people talking about the *solemn truth*, begging others to *tell me the truth*, because *truth is important*, and *the truth cannot be misrepresented*.

But is truth really more important than anything else?

From what I can tell in my limited experience of life so far, more often than not the truth causes damage. The most trivial "fact" can pack enough destructive power to blow apart the life of your average person. To say nothing of what we call "the truth", which can be a whole lot crueller than you imagine.

She and I have a whole range of facts we've acquired over time. Existing facts, facts we discovered, and facts we created. But what is the *truth*? Is there any truth between us?

I see Aki sitting here in front of me trying to tell me something. I don't know if it's the truth or not. But I am sure it's an attempt to destroy me.

"I think I was there," she starts off, then sighs.

"'There' being where?"

"In the room above the dry-cleaner's."

"You were there? How come?"

"Because I was being babysat."

"You were?"

"We never lived together when we were children," she states flatly, with a look of conviction.

"What —"

"The child I remember crying was somebody else. Not you. We don't have any memories in common."

My head spins. What is she telling me?

No, I shouldn't kid myself. Even before she started talking, I had my suspicions about the uncomfortable *fact* that might be at the centre of all this. But my mind refused to acknowledge it. I didn't want to know.

"Listen, Hiro, do you really not get it? Do you not understand what I'm trying to say?" she says sharply.

Still I say nothing. Usually I wriggle out of having to say anything definitive. I don't like to be the one responsible for ending things.

She fixes me with that stare, and eventually says quietly, "I died in an accident when I was a child. As it says in the article."

That's so like her, to be the strong woman. It's why I was attracted to her in the first place. Her strength… Now here I am, trying to run away from it. Once again she's the one saying what has to be said. Not me.

"Died? You?" Even now I play innocent. "Who am I speaking to then?"

She is even able to raise a faint smile at this. "As if you don't know. You always do this, don't you, Hiro? Make me be the one to speak."

She sees through me. She knows everything.

"I am Miyuki Takahashi."

With that one sentence, something snapped. The thing connecting me to her, the thing she and I created. It only took a second, but whatever it was vanished, just like that.

Had it been true? Whatever it was we'd had between us?

"Your mother and my mother were both in difficult situations and both had young children. So your mother decided to adopt out her daughter because she was in a bad position, health-wise and financially."

She is choosing her words with care: *your mother, my mother*. We were born of different mothers. Mothers who were sisters.

"I expect she had already made the decision to adopt Chiaki out when the accident happened," she continues, matter-of-factly. "Maybe she had already received money or some other kind of compensation from the adoptive parents. But then Chiaki went out to play one day and never came back. Somehow she managed to get into the nearby construction site and fall down a pit. It was a tragic accident that nobody could have foreseen."

Her instincts have always been excellent. She arrived at the truth before I did. Calm, collected and logical – that's her to the core.

"Mother wouldn't have known what to do. She had already taken the money, and was very likely having difficulty making ends meet. To have to announce that she couldn't give her daughter up for adoption any more would have been a great blow. So she talks it over with her sister. The sister whose husband is dead and in an even worse financial situation. This sister has a daughter she cannot care for by herself as she is ill and bedridden. She relies on the kindness of neighbours. The two of them come to a decision. They will send Miyuki Takahashi off for adoption in place of Chiaki."

Why do her words come to me in snatches, like sound bites from a documentary? They filter into my brain like pieces in a mosaic and settle into place. It's not only her voice, but also all the different images I have of her in different moods that affect me too. They move across my vision in flashback, throwing me deeper into confusion.

She continues: "I don't know what story they cooked up between them to cover the truth. Chiaki's name would have been on the search request. The lady who helped look after Miyuki might have helped them. But somehow they were able to make it look like Miyuki was the missing child, not Chiaki. Maybe they said that both girls went missing together and only Chiaki was found.

"In any case, the girls were around the same age. Their mothers were sisters, so they may have had similar features. I don't know if the adoptive parents had already met Chiaki or not, but small children's faces change quickly, and they may not have noticed that she was not the same girl that they had met before.

"And so Miyuki Takahashi becomes Chiaki Takahashi, is adopted out, and finally becomes Chiaki Fujimoto."

A deep silence falls over us. The thread is broken. There is nothing left to repair it with. Nor do either of us want to.

*

"What do you think of my theory? It explains everything, doesn't it?" she asks after a while with a clear smile. "Why I don't remember you as a child. Or a fancy clock. The daydream I had in the mountains was triggered by a sound like that of the electric fan in the room above the dry-cleaner's," she says, like a chant. "The sound of insect wings. The fan." Now she even seems to be enjoying herself. "You came over to play sometimes, that's the limit of my memories of you. But the memories of the sounds from daily life have always been there deep inside me. On that day they came to the surface." A dreamy look comes over her face. I can all but hear the drone of the electric fan echoing in her head: *bnnnnn bnnnnn bnnnnn.* "The dream can be explained."

She quickly looks down at the palms of her hands. Is she seeing herself as a child burying something?

"There were two Chiakis. That's why I couldn't see a face on the Chiaki playing with Hiro. Although I recognized myself as Chiaki playing with the sand, the real Chiaki was someone else. I wasn't born Chiaki, but I became her – the child in my dream who ran over to play in the sand became Chiaki. I was remembering becoming Chiaki and burying the real Chiaki. And she really did die. But I wasn't the only to bury her, you did too, Hiro, and everybody else. The fact was covered up."

So that's how it was. I am an accomplice too. No surprises there. The substitute Chiaki was probably handed over not long after the accident. Obviously the loss of my other half had been of no great importance to me. I became an only child, and accepted all my mother's love as my due.

"It's amazing how memory works, isn't it?" She looks down at her palms again. Almost like she expects to find her memories inscribed on them. "Who would have thought that a kitchen fan could trigger memories of events a year ago?" She looks at me for an instant, as if not sure whether to laugh or cry. "Amazing."

We stare at each other. It's like I thought: the thread is broken. There is nothing left.

"We're cousins. Not twins."

That's the upshot of all this, and again she's the one to say it out loud. Strangely, I feel relieved. But still... cousins? The word sounds completely foreign. What a joke. It's beyond me to think of us in those terms.

She starts to tremble slightly. I look her in the face apprehensively, but she is giggling. Her shoulders shake until she can't contain it any more and bursts out into artificial-sounding laughter.

For some reason I find this incredibly irritating. "What's so funny?"

The bitterness in my voice takes her by surprise at first, but after a bit she explodes into even more gales of laughter.

I boil over. "Stop laughing. There's nothing funny about this."

"But..." She is crying with laughter now. "It's so ridiculous. All that pain and worry. Trying to read each other. Hahahaha. It was so, so silly and pointless. Hahahaha. When we were cousins all along."

"Shut up."

I must have sounded threatening. She stops laughing and turns serious. She shifts her legs nervously and looks at me in fear.

"Why are you angry?"

I'm not – she's the angry one. Too late I realize my slip-up in creating an opening for her.

She begins to erupt. "Why are you angry?" she spits. "This doesn't change the outcome of anything, does it? I was the one acting out a farce, wasn't I, not you. No, you always wanted to stay in the safe zone, didn't you, you tried not to see anything. Always looking at me to see what I think first, then gutlessly wriggling your way out of things. You never could have worked out that we're cousins. I'm the one with the right to be angry. Not you."

My body reacts to her words with an explosion of hatred the like of which I've never felt before.

22

When he knocks me to the floor, I have a strange sense of déjà vu. As if I always knew this would happen. The moment I saw the glint in his eyes, I was afraid for my life.

I have never seen him so enraged. It's a side I've never seen before, but then I doubt if anyone has. He keeps it locked up tight in that dark room of his that only he has access to.

I remain cool. My own anger is nothing compared to the ferocity of his. But this is going as I expected: tonight he will kill me. I can finish my life as I wished, in front of him, tonight. It will all be over. I can be at peace.

I see myself from above as if this were happening to somebody else.

It's such a banal scene. The love affair gone wrong, so clichéd. I can just imagine how the newspapers will write it up. No doubt they will ascribe it to sibling conflict gone wrong. Although we know now that it should read cousins.

These thoughts flash through my brain in the instant before I become aware of my stinging cheek and the fact that I am lying on the floor. No longer do I see myself from outside; instead I see walls and the ceiling, with the naked light bulb glaring in my eyes.

Contrary to expectation, he doesn't raise his hand again. In fact, he has edged farther away from me and is sitting, firmly planted on the floor, his face a deep red.

Why am I still alive? I ask myself as I lie on the floor feeling deflated. No, violently disappointed would be a more accurate description. My cheek burns where he hit me, but the humiliation of lying there like an idiot, having failed to get him to kill me, is even more painful.

I roll my head to examine him. His head droops and his face is filled with disgust, at both of us no doubt.

Gutless bastard. I stare at him coldly. I'm the one who should be angry. I have the right, he doesn't. He at least could have allowed himself that murderous impulse. That would have been better for me. But no, he never gets his hands dirty. He always has me say the final word and then blocks his ears when he doesn't want to hear.

Sluggishly, I rise to my feet. My head spins from both the blow and the alcohol.

We are cousins. The words stick in my brain. They will not go away.

If we are cousins, then we can marry. It wasn't so long ago that arranged matches between cousins were common in Japan. I even know someone at work who married her cousin.

Nothing had stood in our way. I can't believe it. All that effort, the two of us trying desperately not to cross a line – it was nothing more than farce.

I can't help but give a bitter smile.

My cheek burns even hotter where he hit me, reminding me of the pain, but I smile anyway. I know I have arrived at the truth, all by myself. It all makes sense. My conviction will not be swayed. We were born of different mothers, who were sisters, and grew up separately.

Tiredness overtakes me, and I shift back to lean against the wall. Its coolness is comforting.

Why were we attracted to each other? Maybe blood ties did count for something. What was it that drew us together?

I flick my eyes over him. There sits the man with whom I spent the golden days of my youth and shared a mutual attraction. He sits slumped over his knees with his face distorted by loathing, and an awful thought takes shape: I am rapidly losing interest in him.

I think my feelings began to cool when I realized that he was only a cousin, and that nothing stood in our way any more.

The heart certainly is mysterious.

Our love had burned precisely because there were obstacles. One hears of this, but is that really what my feelings for him amount to? I would never have dreamed that they could evaporate this quickly.

I let my hands drop to the floor and notice the bulge of the knife in my skirt pocket as I do so.

The man who died in the mountains was Hiro's father, not mine. He was not related to me by blood. What a peculiar feeling that gives me. Only a very short while ago I believed him to be my father.

Why did he die?

Once again, my suspicions rise. Only now my attitude is different from when I discussed it earlier with Hiro. I couldn't be any calmer than I am now, and feel as if all the truth in the world were within my grasp.

It does seem highly unlikely that an experienced mountain guide should accidentally fall to his death, from that cliff with the wonderful view. Our conclusion so far is that he was shaken by the possible sudden appearance of his son and wanted confirmation. But why was it necessary to go so close to the cliff edge?

That cliff with the wonderful view… The words ring a bell.

I picture the scene. There was a ravine at the bottom of the cliff that was also part of the route we followed on the trail. We had passed along there when we began our ascent of the mountain. I picture the three of us walking along in single file.

What if somebody had been down there? What if there was someone on the trail at the base of the cliff, who the guide wanted to signal to and convey a message? That particular spot would be the best location. Everywhere else, the trail was surrounded by forest and would not be visible from the bottom of the cliff. That place where we took a rest break would be ideal for someone at the base of the cliff to communicate with somebody else on the mountain.

Cold sweat breaks out, and a shiver goes up my spine. What is this nagging feeling? What am I missing?

What if —

What if the guide knew about the existence of children from his first marriage all along?

A theory suddenly forms. I glance tentatively at my wretched-looking cousin. What if that man and this one have something in common? What if they were alike in being able to casually ignore the facts in front of their noses, to evade responsibility and run away from trouble?

Images of the two men overlap in my mind. They are astonishingly alike. Smart, calm and collected, never getting their hands dirty, always ignoring their own hypocrisy. Both with a keen sense for anything that smells of trouble. The guide suspected that these clients from Tokyo might be his own children. In all likelihood he knew that his former wife had given birth. Already he had some proof in the form of Chihiro's knife, and the cigarette butts were meant as nothing more than corroboration. Merely for his satisfaction, since he probably didn't have the least intention of identifying himself as their father.

This former drifter had owned up to himself and settled down in the area. He had a family to protect and was less self-centred than he used to be, less bold. There was no way he wanted to rock the boat in his current life.

But what if he was not the only one to have noticed something? What if somebody else had realized that he was secretly investigating his clients and became suspicious? What if that person also wondered if his children might be coming?

I can see it clearly: a young woman standing at the bottom of the cliff, holding a baby and looking wildly up at the top.

She had married a man from the city. A man with a past, much of which was unknown to her, but she knows that her husband had previously been married. He appears nervous and cagey about these clients from Tokyo, and seems to be checking them out. The young wife becomes anxious. She is afraid of what the past might bring back. Or, to be more accurate, she is terrified that the past might drag her husband away from her.

She wants to find out what her husband is looking into. With the instinct of a mother protecting her young, she comes to the same conclusion – that these clients coming soon are the children of her husband's former wife.

What will the conversation between them be like? What will happen? She must have felt insecure.

After meeting them maybe her husband will leave her, maybe he will announce he is returning to Tokyo, or perhaps these children will demand money and reduce his new family to poverty, or maybe he will be so moved by seeing his grown-up children that he will leave her to go back with them, abandoning his wife and child again.

Maybe, maybe, maybe.

She is sick with jealousy and suspicion. The last straw is when her husband returns subdued after his first day out with them. The wife becomes even more anxious and beside herself.

The next day, she takes action. She decides to confront her husband at work, with their child in her arms. She demands that he introduce her to the clients from Tokyo. Perhaps she calls him on his phone to tell him this.

What does he do then?

I see him panic. Quickly he decides on an unscheduled break. He has to make sure that the clients are held up somewhere. Maybe we were already close to that area when he received the message from his wife saying that she was at the start of the trail.

He panics. He has to appease her somehow. But it needs to be somewhere away from his two children, so he makes a call to his wife.

I conjure up a vivid picture of him speaking agitatedly into the phone. He must prevent his wife from meeting the children of his ex-wife at all costs. He is not supposed to know of their existence anyway, and has in fact been pretending that for the last two days. He intended to say goodbye without mentioning anything. This is another reason that he must stop his wife from spilling the truth to them. His performance will be ruined and he could be forced into saying things he never intended.

His wife is on her way to the start of the trail, and somehow he has to stop her. He goes to the cliff with the wonderful view – the one spot where the trail is visible – and desperately tries to signal her down below.

He leans forward a little more than he should.

He loses his footing.

He falls.

Right before the eyes of his wife with their baby in her arms.

I picture the scene in detail and shudder, but I cannot stop. I see the horrified expressions on the faces of husband and wife, and the innocent baby witnessing his father fall. Then comprehension dawning on the wife's face as she realizes at a glance that he is gone. Automatically she flees the scene, and I even see her back.

I see it all, in graphic detail.

23

There was an awkward moment at first after my explosion, before self-loathing set in. I could taste it.

I can't believe I hit a woman. And not just any woman, but her of all people. The act can't be taken back. There's no chance she'll have any feelings left for me now.

My hand still tingles where I slapped her on the cheek. The pain isn't going away, more the opposite. Like a replay is happening in the palm of my hand to match the after-image I still see in my head.

She's flat on the floor, lying still. I guess it's the shock more than pain that keeps her there. What is she thinking? Is she angry? Upset? Feeling disbelief? I'm dreading her looking me in the eye.

Eventually she pulls herself up slowly and turns to look at me.

I watch her out of the corner of my eye. Her hair is a mess but she doesn't tidy it. Her face is blank. I can't figure out what she's feeling.

Where *did* that explosion of emotion come from? Why was I in such a rage?

For a time I can't move either. Or look her in the face. But I feel her eyes boring into me. After a bit I sense a change in her expression and turn to look, without thinking. Her face shows shock and horror. I jump as the horror spreads to me too.

"What's wrong?" I say, instead of the apology that should have been the first thing out my mouth.

"Uh, nothing in particular." She shakes her head dully. I get a sense she's thinking about something else, not me hitting her. "I think I know how your father came to die on the mountain."

"What?" I answer automatically.

Her eyes immediately slide off mine.

"How do you know? Why did he die?"

Your father, not mine, I as good as hear her say. She's acknowledging the established facts.

Still she says nothing.

"Did you remember something?" I demand. If she had some kind of brainwave about his death, I want to hear it.

She looks startled. I see icy contempt in her face, the thing I most feared. My cheeks burn.

"Why don't you think for yourself for a change? He's *your* father, and you're a lot like him."

My face burns even hotter at her cold tone. "I wouldn't know that."

"Oh? I saw a resemblance. Try putting yourself in his position, imagine what he might have thought and done." The contempt is gone from her voice. Now she sounds indifferent, like she's beyond caring. Her face looks resigned, as if this has nothing to do with her.

I try to keep my anger in check. "It's all very well for you to think this is nothing to do with you," I snap. "But this is about my father. If you have any opinion in connection with that, I would like to hear it."

Her eyes go wide and she bursts out laughing. "Oh. My. Goodness."

Again, with some difficulty, I hold back the surge of black rage.

Slowly she shakes her head. "*Like to hear*, would you? *Like* to hear, not *need*? The bottom line is that that's the level of your father's existence for you, isn't it?"

Words stick in my throat.

She keeps shaking her head. "I'm not telling. Anyway, it's only speculation on my part. My wild imagination at work again. Whenever I tell you my ideas you either go into denial or act shocked. But you can't wait to hear me to say these things all the same. You must hate it when I come out with another one of my awful ideas. You already hate me for saying things you don't want to hear about."

"That's not true." But I know she's right. It takes everything I have not to let her see how much it gets under my skin to hear her say what is, essentially, correct. "I'm not angry. Do please enlighten me," I plead, trying to put what little sincerity I have left into the words. But now she's shown me her indifference, she merely flicks me a glance.

"I'm not telling you."

"Don't be such a tease."

"I don't want you to hit me again."

Remembering that I haven't said sorry yet, I quickly bow my head in deep apology. "I'm sorry. It was wrong. I didn't mean to get rough. Truly."

"Hmm. Actually, you *are* a violent person," she murmurs.

"Me?"

"Yes. I've always thought so."

"I'm not violent," I protest hotly.

"But you hit me."

"And I apologized for it. I was upset about a lot of things – I'd just learned the shocking truth."

"Oh yes, so it's my fault, is it? That's exactly why I'm not telling you any more of my theories." She sighs.

I can think of numerous excuses, but suddenly feel unsure. Maybe she is right, maybe I *am* violent.

She looks me in the eyes and says nonchalantly, as if she's just thought of it, "Tell me, Hiro, have you ever loved anybody? Truly loved, I mean, from the heart?"

For a beat my heart goes still. Of all the surprises I've had tonight, this one blindsides me the most. Have I ever loved anybody?

Her eyes seem vacant. Has she already lost all feeling for me, or does she think I never loved her to begin with?

I'm surprised by how upset the thought makes me. How much it pains me. But I can't answer her question, because I can't say with any confidence that I ever have loved anybody.

I don't remember what Misako looks like any more. She's as real as someone in a faded old photograph. I can't believe I'm leaving here to go and live with her.

Aki is lost in her own world. She doesn't appear to expect me to answer. She is staring at a point on the wall with her arms wrapped round her knees under the skirt.

Suddenly I feel exhausted. I'm tired of this emotional ping-pong, the self-disgust and my own stubbornness. This night has been way too intense. What the heck are the two of us doing here? I slide to the floor and feel the tatami stick to my sweat.

My mood turns reckless. If only the world would end now, and this room was the last place of safety left. The outside world would be in cinders but we'd be the only two who don't realize it's the end of the world. Then I could just stay here lying on the floor forever and rot away.

"I remembered the last scene of that movie," she says.

"Huh?"

"The movie I was talking about before. You know, the university students in a room who compete to see who can stand the gas the longest."

"What happened in the end?" I ask, mechanically.

"Eventually everybody runs away. The final scene is a girl going out into the street at night. A sad ballad plays, and that's the end."

"Huh. How boring."

"Yes, isn't it."

This seems like the first time we've agreed on anything in a while.

"So boring," she says, and glances over at the kitchen. "I wonder how long it takes to gas yourself."

"In a large room it'd be pretty difficult. A hose attached to a car exhaust is more reliable. Plus if you use the town's gas supply and it ignites or explodes, it wouldn't be good for the neighbours."

"You're right. You'd have to feel sorry for the landlord too. Nobody would want to live in an apartment where the previous tenant committed suicide."

"You could seal up the room and burn coke briquettes. Carbon monoxide poisoning. I don't think that'd cause an explosion."

"Aha, the favourite method of would-be suicides who go online to find other people to do it with."

The conversation continues automatically, out of habit, but I see a faint spark of interest in her eyes.

"What would everyone think if you and I died here together?"

"From carbon monoxide poisoning?"

"Anything. If the two of us were found dead the morning that we were supposed to leave here, I wonder what people would say?"

I picture us lying on the floor. The scene somehow feels very real. We are lying in similar poses right this minute.

"Suicide? Murder?"

"Too ambiguous."

"I wonder. Grown weary of life doesn't sound right."

"What reason could there be for a twin brother and sister to carry out a suicide pact?"

"I wonder."

I bet we both have the same thought. To consummate forbidden love. We'd never say that out loud, of course. It's strange how the sense of oneness we used to have feels like it's coming back. This night has been a long battle of wits. We're both tired out and at some point have gone back to being our usual selves. The strain of the last few months has vanished. We're friends and allies again.

"I'm tired. Aren't you?" she says.

"Yeah."

"Shall we die together?" she suggests with a smile.

A thrill runs through me. Right then her smile is so beautiful it hurts.

24

I had a boyfriend in my first year of high school who was a kind, clean-cut sort of person. But looking back now, I think the only reason I liked him was that he liked me. I went out with him because I liked him liking me, not because *I* actually liked *him*.

At the time, though, I did enjoy seeing him. My heart beat faster and I believed that I was in love. But it's hard for young teenagers to know what real love is. I behaved how I believed that a girlfriend ought to behave. I said the things that I thought he wanted to hear, and I looked at him the way I thought he wanted me to. I believed I was being sincere. I was convinced that it was love.

Now I know that a person can tell instinctively if the other is responding to feelings of affection honestly or not. This boy eventually realized what I was doing and after a while couldn't take it any more. He began to mention it at every opportunity, trying to call me to account. I was confused by his attitude and I couldn't understand why on earth he was finding fault with me. So I became more and more defensive until eventually things soured between us and we broke up.

Why am I thinking of this all of a sudden? Why now,

after I have just proposed a suicide pact with a man I know I'll be saying goodbye to in a few hours?

Hiro's personality is nothing like my high school boyfriend's, who truly was very understanding and thoughtful for his age. They are completely different in appearance too. But now that the two are joined in my mind, I can't seem to shake the thought of my former boyfriend.

I can still see him standing and staring at me on a cold winter's day, with a scarf wrapped around his neck. Looking at me with a quiet, steady gaze. Criticizing me. His eyes saying: *You don't have to pretend to like me any more.*

I recall his exact words: "Hey, enough's enough. You don't have to bend over backwards pretending to like me." I was outraged by what I took to be spite. How could he say such a thing when I had always been so cheerful and nice? When I'd done so much for him? I was confused by the sadness and resignation in his eyes.

A chill ran through me as the scales fell from my eyes. Of course. I had simply accommodated myself all along and given a performance. When he called me out on it my angry reaction was also pretence, a cover for the guilt and embarrassment. I turned discomfort into anger in order to deflect the indignity of having the cruelty of my actions and hypocrisy pointed out.

I am doing it again now. I don't love Hiro either, I have simply been going through the motions, flattering and trying to please him all along.

When I said "Let's die together", there was no mistaking the glee in his eyes. I feel guilty: he probably thinks I have forgiven him when I haven't. I simply don't care any more. But still I keep flattering him, a man I don't love who is about to go off with another woman tomorrow – no, not tomorrow, today. Why do I keep doing this? Why do I try to please him, when all it does is make me disgusted with myself? Am I afraid of not being liked?

Hiro opens his mouth to speak. "Aki, if it means I can be with you, let's do it."

Hah! He's doing the same as me! He's flattering me too. I don't have to be guilty any more. Who's to say that the glee in his eyes wasn't genuine? After all, I used to be capable of putting on a smiling, vivacious face for my boyfriend when I thought I was in love. I could make my eyes ooze affection at will as I stared soulfully into his.

Being adults, Hiro and I are probably better at acting than when I was a teenager. Naturally we want to make our exits in a manner that leaves each of us feeling good about ourselves. Maybe the fact that I'm even thinking this is a sign that I have grown up. Inside, I smile at myself.

If I were younger, I might have been able to let the emotions of the moment carry me along, and throw everything away. Or I might have been capable of ending our relationship with a single stroke and leaving on the spot. But the older one gets, the harder it is to do that kind of thing. All manner of compromises and calculations must be taken into account, and above all the fear of loneliness is real. If a few sad memories and hurt feelings are the sole price, then closing one's eyes to the other's faults and curling up in retreat is easy enough to do.

Adult wisdom is the wisdom to protect your heart.

We stare into each other's eyes as we always have, still keeping up appearances. All along we have been accomplices, pretending not to know what is on the other's mind. Suddenly the question I put to him rebounds on me: *Have you ever loved anybody?*

Have I? Did I love Yuji? Did I ever love Hiro? Was that really love? Perhaps I am simply repeating my mistakes. Maybe even now I am doing what the boy in the scarf tried to make me confess to on that day so long ago.

Hiro breaks eye contact and lies down on the tatami. "Death plays an amazing role in the system, you know," he says.

"I don't doubt it," I reply. As his collaborator I can play the part. I know how the dialogue should go.

"Eternal youth isn't that interesting actually." He stares up at the ceiling for a while before continuing. "Human beings can decide when to die. It's amazing, if you think about it. We can say to ourselves: I'm going to die. Isn't that profound? To have death as a choice in your life."

"I wonder if it's true that the mass suicide of lemmings is only a myth."

"Ah, yeah, that was the conclusion in some recent research, wasn't it?"

"So what would you call them all jumping off a cliff into the sea – a bungee jump? Surely not?" I flippantly reply, more out of habit than anything, and I look him in the eye without thinking.

He gives this serious consideration. "Could be."

"A bungee jump?" I repeat, and he nods.

"What about insects that jump into the fire in summer? They're attracted to the light and move of their own accord, but you wouldn't call that committing suicide, would you?"

"No, of course not. But they do throw themselves at it. I wonder why?"

Automatically I glance at the street light in the park.

"I don't know why," he continues, "but in that moment, when they fly into the flames, they are probably in ecstasy. In short, that's what it is," he says.

"What is?"

"When it comes down to it, dying is just one of the many choices in life. Life and death aren't separate things – death is simply a part of life. That's how it seems to me anyway."

"All right, I understand when you put it like that. I can accept it well enough. But doesn't that put suicide in a positive light?"

"Nope, I'm being neutral. All I'm saying is, it's one choice. Senseless deaths that aren't suicide happen all the time."

"Yes, that's true."

I am here now because a little girl died falling into a pit on a construction site. And Hiro is here because he was given life by the man who fell off the cliff and the woman in hospital whose life is ebbing away. We are here together right now because of countless choices that were made but which we had no part in deciding.

If everything in life is a choice, then what does it mean to love a person? If love is merely a means for genes to satisfy a self-interested desire for descendants, then surely physical desire is enough for the purpose?

Perhaps love is a mechanism to ensure that helpless, immature human beings are cared for after coming into the world? But ultimately that, too, would make it all about securing descendants. As proved by a love that has nowhere to go or cannot be consummated, love cannot simply be a means of ensuring survival.

"So... death is a form of life?" I murmur.

As I say this, I absolutely relate to the idea. I'm exhausted, the future is shrouded, everything feels like too much trouble, and all I can do is dance the same dance with him, unable even to be disgusted with myself.

This is *exactly* the time for the temptation of death to come visiting. With a sweet-smelling air of unconcern offering refuge easily within reach. That's the illusion it casts. If only I could get out of here, go over to the other side, how much easier everything would be. I would find peace...

That's how it starts.

It is becoming clear to me that lovers' suicide is, in some sense, a consummation of life. Nothing could give more of a sense of achievement at having loved than the death of your lover, because it is a denial – with one's life – of the possibility of descendants.

"It's getting light," he says, shifting his gaze while still lying stretched on the floor. "Dawn's coming."

I turn to look out of the window. "The hour when people most want to die."

Sunrise comes early in summer. Though it is still dark, I can see a tiny stroke of lightness in a corner of the sky. Morning is in the air. How many other people in the world are experiencing this particular dawn, at this particular moment? How many others will greet its arrival after a long sleepless night of despair, regretting that they are still alive? Somewhere, somebody is bound to be in the process of dying – dying in place of us who cannot die here now.

Or is it possible that we could die too?

I steal a look at him lying with eyes fixed on the ceiling. Apparently his usual mild self has returned. There is no sign of the earlier rage. It has gone completely, together with the self-revulsion and ecstasy. The cool, intelligent expression I know so well is back in place.

We were so wrapped up in our own hypocrisy and arrogance we just might have managed to pull off killing ourselves simply to justify the consummation of a forbidden love. The truth is, however, that we don't love each other. Maybe it was merely self-love that we saw reflected in the other, but if we had succeeded in borrowing the power of the night, we might have been able to make it real.

Temptation. This was the temptation. To imagine it. Not to carry it out. In real life, things rarely finish dramatically. Most of the time a vague and inconclusive ending awaits us.

Will tonight be any different?

I curl my fingers around the knife in my pocket.

25

Summer mornings come early. Once you notice, it's already getting lighter by the minute, forcing an end to the night.

My back is stiff, and I feel the kind of tiredness I get from pulling all-nighters. It feels unnatural to be upright and makes me realize why the human body is designed to spend several hours a day lying down.

The night certainly went by fast. It feels like we've been on a very long trip. It seems like an eternity since we spread the food on the suitcase and started drinking. I've been through every kind of emotion since. Suspicion, fear, anger, regret. All in one night.

I can't explain my state of mind now. It's weird – a strange mix of conflicting emotions. Satisfied but also edgy, combined with exhaustion that makes me feel, I don't know, resigned in a way but also somehow high.

What did we resolve? And what didn't we resolve? I can't make sense of it any more. I'm not sure I care either.

What is clear, though, is that morning brings back sanity and puts an end to all the manoeuvrings and intrigues of the night. Morning is neutral. It puts everything back into ordinary perspective. The shine has gone off things that were vitally important just a few hours ago, and now they seem trivial and cheap.

In my current frame of mind, a suicide pact with her is still on the table. The attraction of it is balanced out by its sheer pointlessness. My thoughts and emotions have run together and flattened out. It's difficult to concentrate and think.

Something in the corner of my vision catches my eye. The only possession of ours left in the room apart from the suitcase. We've been avoiding the topic of it all this time, and the question of what to do with it remains undecided.

"Aki, what about that?" I mumble, jutting my chin in its direction.

She looks tiredly at the photo stand. It's an arty kind of thing, with a clock inset in the corner and gaps for several photos. Quite classy. The frame is amber-coloured parquetry that neatly hugs the curved line of the glass. We found it at a gallery not long after moving here and fell in love with it. It was a lot more expensive than we'd expected, but we liked it because it's a work of art in itself. In the fever of the moment, we went halves in buying it as a memento of moving in together. We still had stars in our eyes then.

Neither of us ever regretted buying it. It looks good in this apartment, and we've never got sick of the design. We liked to put our holiday snapshots in it and look at them while talking about where to go next. The clock was useful for telling the time too. It was like we had someone watching over us.

Now it's pushed up against the wall in a corner, looking lonely and abandoned. The photo slots are empty and the clock has stopped. We gave up putting snapshots in it after the trip to the mountains last year, and neither of us could be bothered replacing the clock battery. It became like a part of the wall.

The empty gaps in it made the trip hard to get out of my head. I kept seeing what should have been there. The lack of photos only triggered my imagination, and I replayed everything in my head in detail. The sharp, piercing sunlight. The overgrown mountain trails. The forest's powerful presence. The smell of grass under our feet. Those memories were a torture and kept me trapped.

In retrospect I see how looking at those stark, empty gaps every day gradually changed us. They ate away at us so that bit by bit we turned into something completely different. At some point we noticed the clock had stopped, but neither of us said anything. Before that trip we would have talked about it and said, *Hey, the clock's stopped, I'll change the battery,* or something like that.

After we decided to move, the photo stand was never mentioned. Not even after we started packing up. We divvied up all our other knick-knacks and objects and the apartment gradually emptied, but nothing happened with the stand. It simply stayed there looking sad. It's too expensive to throw away, too well used to sell second-hand, but not old enough to be antique. I don't have the heart to give it to a stranger, but it's too painful for either of us to take it. I think each of us secretly hoped the other would take it, and we were still coming to terms with the idea that one of us would. So now it's still there, after everything else has been packed up and taken away. Even after the sideboard it stood on went.

"What shall we do?" she says blearily, with her eyes still on it. "Leave it here? I don't want to throw it out, even less sell it." She turns to me with a blank expression.

It's like I thought: she'd been thinking the same as me. "We could leave it in a cupboard," I say. "But there's bound to be someone coming to clean before the next tenant moves in, so most likely it'll get tossed out."

"Probably. But they might also take it and sell it on to a second-hand dealer." She speaks in a low voice, without emotion.

"Imagine what the next tenant would think if they came in and found an empty photo stand. Creepy. I'd chuck it out without a second thought, no matter how valuable it looked."

"Yes. You would wonder what photographs it used to hold and why the owners left it behind."

And that is the crux of our problem. The reason we can't decide what to do with it. When we think about the photos it used to hold, and the ones it might have, neither of us feels up to taking it. We stare at it propped against the wall. It's almost like there are still photos in it. As if it holds the thing we've lost.

On impulse I reach over and touch it. It feels heavy and solid as I gently drag it towards me.

"Are you going to take it, Hiro?" she asks, hopefully.

"Er, I haven't decided yet. I just had a thought."

I turn the stand over, jiggle the metal tabs and open up the back. Then I take the photo from the pages of my notebook, insert it in the middle gap and replace the back. An image of me, her and him now fills the centre of the emptiness. It was taken by another tourist during our trek – the first and last shot of the three of us together. Looking at it now, I see us, looking out from the past to our future selves. Just like the old photograph I saw on the book cover in the bookstore.

We look completely different trapped beneath the glass and enclosed in a fancy parquet frame.

She's right. We look like one happy family. Out in the great outdoors, on a beautiful day, relaxed and having a wonderful time. But it was only a fairy tale from a long time ago, in another world. The fictitious scene is encased forever, like a guarantee that we had once been happy.

"I think I get it," I say.

"Get what?" she asks.

"Everybody smiles for photos, don't they? In school or group photos, people automatically smile when they look at the camera. Albums are full of people smiling. But if that's the only kind of photo you see of the past, your memory of it gets distorted. You fall under the illusion that everything was always happy and lightness when it fact it wasn't. There's always some kind of conflict going on behind the scenes – people being bullied, love-hate relationships playing out and so on."

We both smile.

We are looking at the camera. Looking at ourselves, looking at this photo in the future. Looking so we can tell ourselves that the past was not so bad. We are always the accomplices of our future selves when we look into a camera with a smile on our face.

All the despair, animosity, fear and resignation hidden behind those smiles is abandoned. We forget. Through the camera we smile at ourselves in the future. Applying the filter of time so that everything might become part of a sweet past. Transformed into a happy memory.

She yawns, sweetly. Innocently, like a child. "Mind if I lie down for a bit?" Even as she speaks she is lowering herself to the floor.

"Go ahead. You can get three hours in if you take a nap now."

"What about you, Hiro?" she asks, rubbing her eyes.

"Yeah. It might be hard to stay awake until the tradesmen arrive. Don't know if I can sleep, but I'll lie down anyway."

"What shall we do with this? A photo in it makes all the difference," she says, glancing at the photo stand.

"Let's think about it when we wake up."

"Good idea."

The straw of the tatami feels a bit sticky when I stretch out on it. I will never feel this tatami again. Through the window I see the morning getting stronger. It won't be long before night loses the upper hand. Birdsong sounds like the arrival of reinforcements.

I close my eyes, but sleep won't come. Already it's too bright, and I know that the hands of the clock can't be turned back to night.

When you think about it, the sun arrives with incredible brutality. Everything gets remade under the force of that brightness. Everything. Like the smiley faces we direct at the camera. It all becomes bright memory. The whole world turns bright.

The thought fills me with despair. But I know that this too will disappear when I get up and go out into the morning. Not long now, just a bit longer.

Lying on the tatami, quietly waiting for the arrival of morning, I am in utter despair but at the same time utterly relieved.

26

In all likelihood this has been the story of a photograph.

I gaze dimly at it in the centre of the frame from my sprawled position on the tatami. The stand we used to look at every day, in which all our time together was inscribed. And the photograph of myself, him and his father, with our fake smiles and fake blood ties.

For one night only, the three of us were acting out a comedy. One of these three is no longer in the world, but he undoubtedly played a crucial role in this night. Yet although his shadow has been between us for a long time, with the arrival of morning I sense it finally leave.

Yes, it was a comedy all along. One person's tragedy can be comical to a viewer, but for the players in this one it was also farcical from beginning to end. Which was frustrating and ridiculous, far too serious, and rather precious.

Here comes morning. Even with my eyes closed I can tell it's almost upon us. Morning brings release. It puts an end to indecision and hesitation, it sends packing all those things we can never make up our minds about. The arrival of the sun is a signal that time is up.

There is a dull ache behind my eyes. Time is up for us. Our last remaining moments have run out.

I see flickering light. Is it the light bulb or the morning sun?

Presently it resolves into sunlight filtering through trees. I see three people walking through deep green forest in the mountains. Bathed in shadow and light, the pretend family walk determinedly along a mountain path, making bright remarks to each other.

I cannot tell if this is dream or fantasy, but in it we are a family. Finally together again after many years, smiling, laughing and chatting to fill in the long blank.

We never dreamed you'd actually be our guide.

Well, we might have secretly hoped. But there are lots of mountain guides.

Actually, I had a feeling it might happen.

So what do you think? Are we what you expected?

No, I didn't know what to expect. Especially since you arrived looking so grown-up.

Our reunion was a complete coincidence too. We both joined the tennis club at university and were paired for doubles. He didn't seem like a stranger at all. I had never experienced anything like it.

She's right. And to be honest, we misinterpreted that for a while. We thought maybe we'd found our soulmates.

Whoa, that's amazing! Good thing you didn't make that mistake.

Yes, it certainly was. But it was a big surprise to find out that we had a little brother much younger than us.

If you'd like, drop by home. You can meet him.

Really? That would be lovely.

Phew, it's hot even in the shade. I'm so out of shape. It's sad.

If we do this leg in one go, after that it's not too bad.

The dappled sunlight is beautiful. It's like being at the bottom of the sea here. I wonder if this is how fish feel when they look up at the surface.

Green rays of light flicker and waver. Three people stand at the bottom of the water, gazing up at the light on the surface. An innocent yearning shines in the eyes of all three, for the faraway surface that cannot be touched. They stare in silence at the unreachable light, at a future that will never arrive.

My bleary eyes open to the blinding glare of the bulb. I rub them and rise to switch off the light. The room immediately feels cooler, and I notice that it is not completely dark any more. Outside it is getting light.

I glance out of the window, then turn to look at Hiro lying motionless, sprawled across the floor. He could be pretending, but I think he really is asleep.

Then I turn to the photograph stand and study those three smiling faces in the dim light. Already, the process of painting over memories has begun. These three people are the family whose reunion I pictured. Who were trekking in the mountains to renew family ties and fill in the blanks of time.

Yes, and when he and I return from that trip we often look at the photo and talk about it.

I'm so glad we went.

You can say that again. I never thought he'd be so friendly to us.

I feel sort of flat now. I was so excited before we went, but now it's as if I don't care any more.

Yeah. To be honest, I thought meeting our father would be more of a drama, but it was over before we knew it. But I feel better now. When I didn't know anything about him I only thought the worst.

Yes, it's as if it doesn't matter any more. And he has a new home and family. I was surprised at myself for being happy for him.

Cute baby, hey.

His wife seemed nice too.

The trekking part was hard work, but I'm glad we decided to do it.

Me too.

I smile at this vision of the two of us sitting with our arms propped on the table, resting our cheeks on our hands as we chat cheerfully.

My legs seem to move of their own accord. I rise to my feet and creep to the entrance, put on my shoes and go outside.

Once out of the door, my feet stop. All of a sudden I am overwhelmed by a sense of freedom. I had forgotten how big the world was out here. For the last few years, the apartment has been everything to me. Taken aback, I swivel my head, taking in scenery that should be familiar but which I realize I have never properly looked at before.

The humidity is not so different to inside, but it does feel slightly cooler out here. With a light head I walk over to the park, which is so still and quiet that it doesn't seem real. It could almost be part of an exhibit where touching is forbidden. I seat myself on one of the two swings and look at the one beside it. The one where he used to sit for our long talks. It is empty.

Without thinking, I reach into my pocket and pull out my phone. My fingers tap out a number that, for some reason, I haven't been able to delete. To my surprise, it answers on the third ring.

"Hello?"

I can tell from his voice that he too has been awake all night, and he knows it is me calling, which means that he has not deleted my number either.

"Were you awake?" I ask him casually, in the far-off place where he is now.

"Yeah. I was thinking about things."

"Oh."

"How are you?"

"Well, I'm about to move."

"Where to?"

"I don't know yet. I'm staying with a friend for a while. You know her. Kyoko Tamaki."

"Oh yes. The one who works for a trading company." I stare at the clock in the park, the one we always used to look at from the apartment. "I just wanted to say that, um, you were right – I did love him. Though I always denied it." I come out with it abruptly. "But in the end, it was a brotherly kind of love. I mean that I loved him *because* he was my brother. If he hadn't been my brother, I don't think I would have been attracted to him. I don't know if that makes sense…"

He absorbs this in silence. "Hmm. I think I do understand."

"Really?"

"Yeah. I can say now that I do."

"Thank you. That's all I wanted to say. Sorry for ringing at this hour. Are you busy at work?"

"Yeah. Up to the neck. But I'm glad of it." He pauses for a beat. "It distracts me."

We share a silence that only we could understand.

"Take care of yourself. Don't work too hard," I say cheerfully, changing my tone.

"Thanks," he answers immediately. "You too."

"Bye then."

"Bye."

I hang up and the eloquent silence of the morning creeps over me, rising from the ground. I give a small sigh and slowly get to my feet. Our apartment is on the other side of the clock. The time we shared is in there. It feels strange to be looking at it from here, on this side.

It is like looking at a stranger's house. As if there is another him and another me, living in that apartment, in another innocent time.

Unable to move, I stare at the window. The window we left open.

Once again, I felt that I had seen dappled sunlight through the trees somewhere. It was in the mountains. And the three of us were gazing up at the bright sunlight coming through the trees.

No, it wasn't. It was now, and the three of us are looking up at that window. Seeing a time that ought to have existed, and been happy.

*

I realize that I still have the phone in my hand, so I return it to my skirt pocket. As I do, my fingers touch another hard object in there. His knife. I pull it out and study it.

The knife with his name engraved on it. This was an important prop in last night's comedy. Gingerly I pry it open and see a blurred reflection of my face in the metal surface. Driven by a sudden impulse, I crouch down next to the clock pole. I have no idea why, but before I know it all I can think about is digging a hole at the foot of this pole. I will bury the knife here, bury it deep in the earth and then slip away without telling anyone what I have done.

I start to dig. Deeper and deeper. So nobody will find it. The dirt is hard and surprisingly difficult to penetrate. I dig until I am out of breath and my head is empty of all thought. The rich smell of freshly dug earth shoots up my nostrils. A gleam from the knife blade unexpectedly escapes through the covering of dirt.

My hands stop moving and I squint into the sky. Finally, the sun has appeared.

THE END